LITERARY OUTLAW

A PULP FICTION MAGAZINE | ISSUE #6

IN THIS ISSUE:

LITERARY OUTLAW #6
Copyright © 2024 by LiteraryOutlawLLC

Front Cover - Person About to Stab Woman stock illustration | CSA Images
Vacancy | Copyright © 2024 by K. Victoria Chase
How Did You Die? | Public Domain
Death's Stagecoach | Public Domain. Originally published in *The Ghost Rider #2*
Legendarium | Copyright © 2014 by Michael Bunker & Kevin G. Summers
Fire and Ice | Public Domain
Who Is The Black Cat? | Public Domain. Originally published in *Black Cat Comics #2*
Penrod | Public Domain. Originally published in 1914
Penrod Illustrations by Gordon Hope Grant| Public Domain. Originally published in 1914
Moby Dick | Public Domain. Originally published in *Thriller Comics Library $157*
Nyarlathotep | Public Domain. Originally published in *The United Amateur November 1920*
The Dreams in the Witch House | Public Domain. Originally published in *Weird Tales July 1933*
Page 68 - The Black Man by Jens Heimdahl | Creative Commons Attribution-Share Alike 4.0 International license
Dig Me No Grave | Public Domain. Originally published in *Weird Tales February 1937*

www.literaryoutlaw.com

VACANCY
BY K. VICTORIA CHASE

Leave him there."

My sister's plea to walk away from Harry had been playing on repeat in my mind for the last hour. Ever since I suggested we stop to have dinner. *I'm not hungry yet; let's keep going,* he had said. The point of this spontaneous road trip was to *save* our marriage. Not unravel the last few strands holding it together.

"Lottie, we're at a gas station in the middle of nowhere Texas. There's no Uber."

The door chimed. A cheerleader walked in flanked by a pock-faced boy sporting a hoody with the same school colors. The boy made a beeline to the bathroom and waited outside while the girl passed me on a mission.

"Where's Harry now?"

I looked over my shoulder. Harry exited the bathroom, smoothing the front of his tucked-in shirt. Even on vacation he dressed business casual. Why couldn't he just relax? Harry spotted a package of jerky on a shelf between us and scanned the back of the bag. "Looking at jerky."

"Ew. Gas station food."

The cheerleader picked up a bag of plantain chips. How'd I miss those?

"I know," I said. "If he had just stopped, like I said."

I moved closer to the girl and reached for the bag of chips in her hand. "Excuse me, sorry. Do you mind if I take those? I've got food allergies." When her grip weakened, I plucked them from her hand.

Her gaze scanned me, and she smirked. "I don't need them anyway." She sashayed towards the bathroom, skirt swinging.

"Who was that?" Lottie asked.

"Some cheerleader who could lose ten pounds."

"How are you handling Harry? What did your therapist say?"

Hmm, how should I handle a control freak? "Not go on a road trip," I mumbled.

"What?"

"She suggested we separate."

"Wait, a minute. When was this?"

"Months ago." I scanned the nutrition label on the plantain chips and then spotted wasabi peas.

"Then what's the point of this trip?"

"He wants to keep trying. And what am I gonna tell Mom and Dad? You know they didn't want me to marry him."

"With good reason."

"I'd forgotten. You didn't want me to marry him, either."

Harry ambled over. "Gotta go." I disconnected the call.

"Was that your sister?" I pushed past my crossbody and shoved my phone into my back pocket. "Are you at least defending me?"

I miffed. "What makes you think we're talking about you?"

"Guinevere said to keep our issues inside our marriage."

Guinevere. Our therapist. "Dr. Patterson, you mean?"

"Find anything?" he asked about the food in my hands. He snatched a family size Doritos bag off the shelf and smiled at me.

I blew out a breath, frustrated. "You know I can't eat any of this."

He dragged a hand down the side of his face. "Kelly, it's just for one night."

"I suggested we stop—"

"The whole point of this was to be spontaneous. To get back to the way things were before." He threw the red bag of chips onto the shelf and grabbed the blue one. His hard gaze held mine. "Isn't that what you said you wanted?"

My voice was clipped. "I have SIBO. A spontaneous dinner at a gas station is going to leave me in pain all night!"

"And Applebees is any better? It's too late to turn back." He sauntered toward the front of the store, stopping at the cashier's desk.

I stared at the items in my hands. Plantain chips and wasabi peas. I chose the chips.

"And where are we going to stay?" I said when I reached the counter. "Because I'm not staying at that motel down the street." The cashier's gaze darted between my husband and me. "We might as well go back. Pretty sure there was a decent hotel. You know, the ones that serve breakfast?"

Harry rolled his eyes and faced me. "It's twenty minutes. We could probably find something up the road in twenty."

"There's a B&B up the road," the cashier said. My gaze snapped to him. He nodded. "Just off the highway." He hooked a thumb behind him. "About half a mile up."

"Are you serious?" I asked him. A B&B sounded like a better option than the we'll-keep-the-blue-light-on-for-you motel. And more romantic.

Because that was the point.

To rediscover what we had lost.

"Yup. The old farmhouse. Used to be the Jenkins' place until this old couple came down a few years ago and bought it. For their retirement. They come in here now and then. Nice people."

I smiled triumphantly at my husband as skepticism circled the irises of his eyes. "Is 'off the highway' spontaneous enough for you? And it's a farmhouse. They'll probably have something organic I can eat."

"Kel, I think we should check in at the motel. It's right here."

"Yeah, miss that farmhouse." We looked behind us at the pock-faced kid and his cheerleader. The boy spoke again. "That couple's crazy."

"Yeah. Crazy," the cheerleader echoed.

"What do you kids know about it?" the cashier said. "What are you two even doing here? The high school's back up the road."

Pock-Face held up candy. "This is the only gas station that has my Mambas."

Harry looked at his watch. "It's ten-thirty. They're probably closed."

The cashier shook his head. "Truckers stop by there all the time. At all hours. They'll be up."

Harry's face twisted in annoyance as he stared down at the cashier. "Fine," he grumbled and stomped out of the convenience store.

I looked back at the kids. "Old people are always crazy."

Pock-Face shook his head.

We almost missed the turn off the highway. The B&B sign sat far back from the road. I saw it first and nearly yanked the steering wheel because Harry claimed he couldn't see it.

Another quarter mile along a lane of thick forest and the lit front wrap-around porch came into view like a lighthouse on the shore during a storm. My lips parted into the widest grin I'd had in a long time.

Then I squealed and squeezed Harry's arm. "Doesn't it look amazing?"

"Is that a cornfield in the back?"

"There's a porch swing. I love porch swings."

"You do?"

"They're romantic and cozy," I said.

"We've never sat on a porch swing."

I had with my high school sweetheart, but I swallowed those words. Harry hated when I brought up exes like a measuring stick. "Porch swings in the city? We need a *house* for that."

"Our condo has appreciated five percent last year." Harry pulled up the gravel driveway and turned off the car. He stared at the house, uncertainty growing with in every new crease in his brow.

"What are we waiting for?" I asked, eager to get inside as my stomach growled.

"Where are the trucks?"

"Huh?" I looked around. "Trucks?"

"Yeah. The cashier said truckers are usually here. Where are they?"

I rolled my eyes. "Maybe there'll be a trucker here later. Who cares?"

He looked at me like I wasn't thinking straight. "If no one's here, there's a reason. Maybe this place is worse than the motel."

I opened my door. "No place with a porch swing is worse than a motel. Get our bags. I'm going to check us in." I slammed the door and hurried along the brick walkway to the creaky front wooden steps that reminded me of my grandparents' farm. Oh, the creaking! I shivered in delight.

A small sign posted in the glass front door said Vacancy. I turned the iron antique doorknob and opened the door.

The suitcase slammed into each brick as Harry dragged it along.

"Hello?" I called out as my eyes took in my surroundings. My feet sank into the runner beneath my feet, the large gold, blue, and red flowers beckoning me deeper into the decidedly country farmhouse. Lantern sconces lined the walls, fire flickering around the wick of candles dripping with wax. On either side, doors led to separate sitting rooms.

"Are you from the gas station?"

I jumped at the sound of the voice to my left. Hand over my heart, I saw a woman at the fireplace, jabbing a poker into crackling logs. "You scared me," I said.

Lines etched around the corners of her mouth. She placed the poker on the stand and smiled. "I'm sorry, dear."

"Yes, my husband—he's coming in now—and I were just at the gas station. The cashier said you'd have vacancy."

"We do! You're our first guests of the night."

Harry stumbled through the door with his duffel bag slung over his chest and wheeling my luggage behind him.

"Come right on in," the woman said. "I'm Sandra Lehman. My husband, Bill, is around here somewhere. Probably fixin' the plumbing in one of our baths. Old farmhouses often need repairs. How 'bout you set those down and I'll have Bill take them up to your room."

Harry grasped the strap of his duffel bag and tightened his grip on the handle of my bag. "I got it."

Sandra arched a brow at me as if to say she understood my secret pain. "Just for one night?"

"Yes," I said. "You wouldn't happen to still have any—"

"Dinner? Oh, yes. We keep a pot of soup on the stove for late arrivals. And I can whip up a salad and sandwiches if you prefer."

"A sandwich for me would be great," Harry said. He gestured toward me. "Soup for her, if it's vegetable."

"We grow our own in the backyard. And we have chickens for eggs in the morning. How would you like them?"

I grinned. "Over easy."

"Scrambled," Harry said.

"We'll have a variety of gluten-free breads with homemade jam, yogurt and granola, and my husband loves a country breakfast—bacon and potatoes."

"I'll take all of that," Harry said, his eyes wide with hunger.

"Follow me and I'll check you in," Sandra said. She walked into the sitting room on the right.

Harry waited for me to go in first. "Still want to go back to the motel?" I asked under my breath before lifting my nose and entering the room.

"Whoa!" Harry called out. He lifted his leg and stared at the rug on the floor.

"Don't mind the dip," Sandra called. "These old wood floors... That's on Bill's fix-it list." Harry stepped over the sag I had missed when I walked inside.

Sandra stood behind a wooden desk. Her fingers flew across the keys of a sleek, newer model laptop. "You two look like newlyweds. We have a discounted rate."

"No!" Harry and I said in unison. I chuckled nervously and smiled, our aggressive negation eliciting a wide-eyed, open-mouthed host. "We've been married for five years."

Sandra's smiled appeared forced. "Kids?" Her eyes going to the door expecting to see tiny humans entering.

"No way," Harry answered.

"My husband and I could only have one. Jackson. He'll stop by from time to time. But our guests are like our children. We cook for you, clean if you need it, and give you advice about the area."

"How sweet," I said, unsure how to respond. Harry and I couldn't agree on anything except not having kids. We wouldn't want to bring innocents into our dysfunction.

Sandra held up a card reader. "Just tap," she said cheerfully. "We have all the latest tech." I tapped our credit card. "Okay, all set. You'll be in the Ranchero room. Back of the house on the east side. It's the largest room in the house!"

Within five minutes, we were upstairs grinning at the king bed with fresh, crisp white linens. Bill must've run up here while we were checking in because on top of the plush duvet sat a tray with a bottle of chilled wine in a metal bucket and bowls of chocolate, strawberries, and some cookies.

An aged floral rug slinked out from beneath the bed, covering most of the creaking oak floors. Candles flickered on the wall sconces, creating a romantic ambiance. Our minimalist bedroom back home lacked the warmth of this charming suite.

My heart trembled with pain. How had we let our marriage grow so rigid? Was it too late? Could we recover what we once had, or was it all an illusion?

"Okay, I admit it," Harry said. "You were right. This place is amazing. And did you smell the soup on the way up? I can't wait to eat. I might become a vegan after this trip."

Goosebumps peppered my arms as I watched an unfamiliar emotion travel across my husband's eyes. Respect? Regardless, the concession was enough to lift my spirits, along with the smell of the soup.

"Thank you," I said.

He smiled. "You're welcome."

Who are we?

Harry took a bite of a cookie. "What fruit is this?" Blood red juice ran down his chin.

I picked up a cookie. "Looks like cherries."

"Doesn't taste like them."

"Is it good?"

He ran a finger up his chin, catching the juice. "Delicious."

"Dinner's ready, if you'd like to come down," Sandra said from the doorway. She grinned, wagged her brows, and disappeared.

"Man, those two are like ninjas. Did you hear her come up? I didn't," Harry said with a shake of his head. He rubbed his hands together. "Soup!" he exclaimed.

I didn't hear her because I was too busy rediscovering the shimmering ocean in his eyes.

SANDRA DIPPED A SLATE GRAY LADLE into the pot atop a sunflower potwarmer in the center of the table. "Come on in and have a seat. It's hot."

We slipped into our seats. "Is someone joining us?" I asked about the third bowl.

Sandra placed a hand on her chest. "Me! I hope you don't mind. After smelling this for hours, there's no way I'm not eating a bowl. Bill might join us later when he's finished in the basement."

"Working this late?" Harry asked.

Sandra grinned. "I married the perfect man. He doesn't have a problem doing little chores here and there whenever we need it." She finished filling her bowl and sat down. "And we're going to be busy soon. A little preparation goes a long way."

"This soup is delicious," Harry said. "What's that flavor? Is it bacon?"

Sandra's laughter floated in the air. "It tastes like bacon, don't it? It's my special blend of spices, a sprinkle of No Bagel Seasoning, and a little tofu."

"Tofu? Really? Tastes better than bacon."

"Thank you, dear," Sandra said.

I chewed on the tofu but found the texture tougher than any brand I had ever tried. Still, it was delicious. I couldn't complain.

After enjoying two bowls, a ham and cheese sandwich, and another three cherry cookies, Harry went upstairs to shower. I stayed to have Sandra read my palm. We laughed as the tip of her finger tickled the sensitive skin of my hand. I sipped on the thickest red wine.

Sandra tsked. "I'm sorry to have to tell you, dear, but Harry is going to leave you."

I coughed as the wine went down. "Excuse me?"

"See how this line splits?" She pointed to the brown line on my hand. "That's the love line. A strong split like this means your marriage will end. Even the married line has a little break."

I snatched my hand back and tucked it underneath my opposite arm. This was a silly game, but I couldn't deny I'd been feeling this way for a long time. "We've been having problems," I revealed. "Not connecting like we did before we married. He resents the success I'm having with my job, even though he's just as busy. This trip was supposed to bring us closer, you know? Some alone time."

"But you can't stand to be in the same car."

"Exactly!"

Sandra offered a sad smile. "Marriage is hard. Tougher even with kids, but Jackson was always such a good boy."

"What's the secret?" I asked about marriage.

"Working together for a common purpose is the only way to succeed."

I took a sip of my wine, the warmth encouraging as it went down. "What's your purpose? You and Bill."

Sandra's eyes brightened with enthusiasm. "To bring comfort and peace to travelers before they journey on."

"SHE SAID YOU WERE GOING TO LEAVE me," I wailed. I stood in the doorway of our bathroom, finishing my wine.

Harry's shoulders slumped, his knees together as he sat on the toilet. He blamed the soup. "That's ludicrous."

"We haven't been happy for a long time."

Harry frowned.

The lights flickered and then everything went dark.

I giggled.

Harry groaned. "Now I've gotta finish in the dark?"

"Hurry up. I want to take a shower."

"That's not helping."

I answered a knock at the door. Sandra stood there, a candle in her hand and a bag in the other. "Sorry about the lights. It happens from time to time. A storm is close. Here's a bag of candles and matches. Let us know if you need more. We have plenty."

"Thank you," I said, taking the bag.

I struggled to light the matches in my inebriated state.

The shower water started, and Harry howled. I ran into the bathroom. "What?"

"The water is freezing!"

"I'll go find Sandra."

With a candle, I descended the stairs, calling out Sandra's name. No response. The house was dark as pitch. I took the hallway toward the kitchen, where I figured Sandra would be. As my eyes adjusted to the darkness, lighting struck, the brightness piercing the inky

cover long enough to reveal the empty kitchen to my left.

I went right. The first closed door I came to was a half bath. I opened the second closed door. A putrid stench had me stumbling back, my hand going to my nose. I lifted the candle and light flooded the room. Something hung across a line strewn from one end of the room to the other. A hutch with a butcher-block countertop rested against the wall in front of me.

Thunder rolled overhead, and my heart pounded. I stepped inside the room. As the strength of the smell dissipated, the familiar odor of old, dried blood hitting the air remained. Chunks of flesh littered the countertop. A hand flew to my mouth. Was that tofu we ate...pig?

A strong gag reflex constricted my throat as bile shot up from my stomach. I slammed the door and stumbled into the kitchen. The large pot sat on the stove.

I marched to it and removed the top. I snatched a large spoon from the counter and scooped the soup. Vegetables toppled over and fell back into the pot. Something oddly round remained. What vegetable was round? I poked it and it bobbled across the spoon. As it rotated, I moved the spoon toward the candle I had placed on the countertop.

The vegetable was white with a large dark spot in the center.

My hand holding the spoon shook first, followed by my arm and then my entire body. By the time I placed the spoon back onto the counter, all its contents had spilled over onto the counter and the floor.

I ran from the kitchen, stumbled up the stairs, and fell into the room just as Harry exited the bathroom.

"Harry," I said, out of breath. "We have to get out of here!"

His brows came together. "Now? Why? What did they say about the lights? The water's still cold, by the way."

"The...soup. The soup! It's...it wasn't tofu!"

"Hmm," Harry said with a shrug. "Still good."

Hot tears coursed down my cheeks. Why wasn't he hearing me? He never heard me anymore. "Harry" I shrieked. "I saw it!"

"Saw what?"

"The meat!"

He rolled his eyes as he pulled his boxer shorts up to his hips. "Eating meat for one night isn't going to kill you."

"It. Was. *Human*!"

Thunder cracked the sky. Harry stared back at me, blinked twice, then howled in laugher. "You're kidding, right?"

I sniffed and shook my head. I scooped up the toiletries I had placed on the bed for my shower and dumped them back into the suitcase.

"What are you doing?"

"You don't believe me."

"Kel, it's pretty ridiculous. I mean, how do you know it was human?"

"This is why we don't work. We're not a team."

"Oh, here we go."

He was always against me. Never on my side. I zipped up my suitcase. "I'm not staying here."

"Kel...Kelly, wait. Calm down. How much wine did you drink?"

I slipped my arm from his grasp but halted at the door. I faced him. The reddish-orange glow from the candles cast shadows across his face, hiding his expression from me. "Are you coming with me or not?"

A loud rap on the door caused me to jump. I stared at it, fear keeping me from opening the door.

"Kelly? It's me, Sandra. I think you might've had an accident in the kitchen. Are you alright?"

I looked at Harry, frantically waving my arms in the air toward the door, silently pleading with him to do something. He shrugged. What could we do?

"Kelly? There seems to be a misunderstanding. I hope you don't think we fed you meat." The doorknob jiggled. The unmistaken sound of a key slipping into the lock caused the blood in my veins to freeze. "I cook a lot of soup," she continued. "I can assure you the bowl you had wasn't what you saw in the kitchen."

I grasped the doorknob to keep her from opening it.

"What are you doing?" Harry hissed in my ear.

"I'm not letting her in," I whispered back.

"Don't you want to leave?"

I did want to leave, but without Sandra or her husband seeing us go. "Can we make a run for it?"

"Make a run for it?" Harry parroted, as though he didn't understand the question.

"I'll hit her with my suitcase and then we run. Do you have the keys?"

"They're on the dresser." He brought them to me.

"Kelly?" Sharon called again with strain in her voice. The doorknob jerked beneath my grip as Sharon attempted to twist it on her side. "Please open the door, Kelly."

"Sorry Sharon!" Harry called out. "We're not decent. But everything's all good."

Seconds passed. The doorknob tension lessened. "Sorry to bother you. Have a good night."

"Thanks, Sharon."

I stared at my husband. "That actually worked?"

"See? Nothing to worry about. You still want to leave?"

"Yes."

Harry sighed. "Let me get my stuff."

Minutes later, I slowly opened the bedroom door. I winced as it creaked. We tiptoed down the staircase. Thunder rolled in the distance. Rain continued to patter the roof. Sharon hadn't bothered to light candles around the home, hiding our escape.

Harry took the lead, ready to throw the suitcase at anyone to distract them. Seeing the hallway to the front door empty, we darted forward. Wood splintered and Harry screamed as he disappeared through the floor.

"Harry!"

I fell on my knees at the edge of the hole. Was this the dip he felt earlier in the evening? I heard rhythmic squeaking. Wood swung in mid-air.

A trap door!

"Harry!"

His groan was faint.

I fumbled for the flashlight on my phone and shined it into the hole. Dust swirled around Harry and funneled up. I swiped to clear it and choked back coughs as it clawed at my throat.

"Harry..." The dust cleared enough for me to see him on the ground in the basement. His right leg twisted at an unnatural angle.

A large figure stood over him and looked up at me. My free hand flew to my mouth, catching a gasp. *Bill!*

My phone's light ricocheted off a long blade in Bill's hand. At the exact moment, Harry noticed it too.

"Kelly...run!" Harry wailed.

"No! Harry--*nooo!!!*" Bill raised the blade and sliced down.

Harry shrieked.

I screamed. Tears streamed down my cheeks. From across the hole, Sandra barreled towards me, swinging a curved blade. I yelled and threw myself toward the door, ducking enough to keep my head, but a sting shot rapidly down my left arm.

Sandra moved around the hole and swung again. I dove into the living room and then scrambled towards the fireplace. I pulled the wrought-iron poker from the toolset and turned.

Unable to stop in time, Sandra impaled herself onto the poker. I shoved hard, forcing the poker deeper into her. Sandra tumbled onto her back, writhing, and gasping for breath.

Harry's screams had stopped. For a second, all I could hear was the rain on the roof and Sandra's last gasps for air.

I crawled to the hole and peered down. Both Bill and my husband were gone.

Run!

Choking back sobs, I opened the front door and leapt off the porch.

Keys! Where are my keys?

I felt around my pockets, but they weren't there.

I must've dropped them.

What was it—a mile to the highway? I took off running toward the road.

Rain slapped my face. My left arm throbbed. Wet jeans weighed my steps as my shoes sunk into the mud.

I ignored the throbbing ache in my arm and forced my knees higher. After running for what seemed like hours, I made it to the highway. Truck lights blinded me. The driver honked the horn and skidded to a halt. I hoisted myself up the steps beneath the passenger door as the driver rolled the window down.

"Please! Help me."

"You out here alone?"

"My...my husband..." I gasped for air, my lungs burning.

The driver looked beyond my shoulder. "Where is he? Is he hurt?"

"He's at the B&B behind me. The owners...they killed him! They're cannibals. I need the police! Do you have a phone?"

"I...it's dead. Dropped it down the toilet in the last rest area. I could drive you to the gas station up the road."

"Please!" I opened the door and slipped into the seat.

He shifted gears.

I settled back against the seat, exhaustion stiffening my limbs. The rumbling noise of the truck pulled at my eyelids. My heart burned in my chest. *Harry...*

"Did you say you were at the B&B?"

My voice cracked. "Yeah."

"What's your name?"

"Oh! I'm sorry. It's Kelly."

"Well, Kelly, you're okay now."

He exited the highway but didn't turn around. "Um, you're not taking the highway back?"

"Shortcut."

Lightning lit the sky. The farmhouse was in the distance to my right. I swallowed. "You didn't tell me your name."

Out of the corner of my eye, I saw him smile.

"Jackson."

THE END

HOW DID YOU DIE?

Did you tackle that trouble that came your way
With a resolute heart and cheerful?
Or hide your face from the light of day
With a craven soul and fearful?
Oh, a trouble's a ton, or a trouble's an ounce,
Or a trouble is what you make it,
And it isn't the fact that you're hurt that counts,
But only how did you take it?

You are beaten to earth? Well, well, what's that?
Come up with a smiling face.
It's nothing against you to fall down flat,
But to lie there -- that's disgrace.
The harder you're thrown, why the higher you bounce;
Be proud of your blackened eye!
It isn't the fact that you're licked that counts,
It's how did you fight -- and why?

And though you be done to the death, what then?
If you battled the best you could,
If you played your part in the world of men,
Why, the Critic will call it good.
Death comes with a crawl, or comes with a pounce,
And whether he's slow or spry,
It isn't the fact that you're dead that counts,
But only how did you die?

— Edmund Vance Cooke, 1903

the GHOST RIDER
FOUR MEN RULED THE CACTUS GAP COUNTRY... FOUR MEN WHO WERE HONEST AND GOOD, USING THEIR WISDOM AND WEALTH TO SPREAD PROSPERITY THROUGHOUT THEIR RANCHLAND. BUT DEATH CAME RIDING THE CACTUS COUNTRY, TOUCHING THESE FOUR, ONE BY ONE — WITH ONLY THE GHOST RIDER AWARE OF THE STRANGE MENACE THAT HELD THE REINS OF —
"DEATH'S STAGECOACH!"
LUKE MORMON OWNED THE BIG HAT-IN-A-BOX RANCH. WITH PLUMP JEB NOLAN, OWNER OF THE PICKETFENCE SPREAD, HE RULED ALL CACTUS GAP WEST OF TOWN...
-AYERS-
HERE'S TO THAT IRRIGATION TROUGH WE'RE PUTTIN' IN, JEB. WE'LL BE ABLE TO STOCK ANOTHER FIFTY THOUSAND STEERS ON OUR RANCHES, ONCE WATER RUNS THROUGH IT!
TOM COLLINS 35¢
25¢
MILES TO THE NORTH, IN A TINY CAVE, A HAND REACHES OUT TOWARD TWO SKULLS, EACH BEARING A NAME...
LUKE MORMON
JEB NOLAN

THAT NIGHT, SHROUDED IN THE DARKNESS, A BLACK STAGECOACH RACES MADLY DOWN THE SLOPING ROADWAY OF THE GAP—
FASTER, FASTER! DEATH COMES THIS WAY, AND NONE MUST STOP IT — FASTER!

THE FIRST NAME ON DEATH'S LIST! TOMORROW OR THE NEXT DAY— LUKE MORMON WILL DIE!

TWO DAYS LATER, LUKE MORMON CRIES OUT SHARPLY...
TARNATION! WHO THREW THAT LARIAT? I'M GOING TO FALL ON THOSE ROCKS! I'LL BREAK MY NECK!

AGAIN THE STAGECOACH OF DEATH HURTLES DOWN THE ROCKY SIDES OF CACTUS GAP! AGAIN THE GRIM, COWLED FIGURE LEAVES A WHITENED SKULL...
DEATH WILL CALL ON YOU, JEB NOLAN! YOU CANNOT ESCAPE YOUR FATE!
JEB NOLAN

PALLID WITH FEAR, FACE WET WITH SWEAT, JEB NOLAN BABBLES HELPLESSLY TO THE OTHER HALF OF CACTUS GAP'S FAMED FOUR: TOM BRENNAN OF THE B-ON-A-RAIL RANCH, AND ROGER BOOFER, OWNER OF THE TRIANGLE-DOT...
LUKE DIDN'T DIE NATURAL. HE WAS MURDERED! I SAW THE SKULL HE GOT! SAME AS THIS — BUT THIS'N HAS MY NAME ON IT. I'M NEXT! I'M NEXT TO DIE!

EASY, JEB! WE'LL THINK O' SOME WAY TO HELP YUH!
CORRECT! STAY HERE TONIGHT, JEB. TOM AND I WILL SOLVE THE MYSTERY OF THOSE SKULLS. LEAVE EVERYTHING TO US!
I'M A MARKED MAN! MARKED FOR— DEATH! NOTHING CAN HELP ME! NOTHING!

RIDING ACROSS THE SAGE FLATS SOUTH OF CACTUS GAP, NEXT DAY, COMES REX FURY, U.S. MARSHAL...
LOOKS LIKE A DEAD MAN LYING THERE! I'D BETTER TAKE A LOOK—!

ODD! HE'S DEAD— BUT THERE'S NO WOUND OR OTHER MARK OF VIOLENCE ON HIM! HOW COULD HE DIE OUT HERE... UNLESS... OF COURSE—THAT'S IT...!

IT'S JEB! HE— HE KNEW HE WAS GOING TO DIE!
HE KNEW IT? BUT HOW? HE HAD ENEMIES, I SUPPOSE?

THIS SKULL WAS LEFT HERE SOME DAYS AGO! A FRIEND OF OURS, LUKE MORMON, ALSO RECEIVED ONE. HE ALSO DIED. AND PEOPLE TALK OF A BLACK STAGECOACH THAT TRAVELS ONLY AT NIGHT...!
THIS HAS ALL THE EARMARKS OF A JOB FOR— THE GHOST RIDER!

UP, SPECTRE! SOMEBODY LEAVES THOSE SKULLS TO BE FOUND BY THE VICTIMS! I WANT TO KNOW WHO IT IS!
AS DARKNESS DROPS LIKE A PALL ACROSS THE PRAIRIE LANDS, REX FURY DISAPPEARS, AND IN HIS PLACE—

AT THAT MOMENT, THUNDERING AROUND A SHARP BEND OF CACTUS GAP MOUNTAIN...
FASTER, MY BEAUTIES! DEATH IS HUNGRY! HE SEEKS MORE MEN TO FEED HIS APPETITE!

A STAGECOACH!...BLACK! AND WITH A STRANGE, COWLED FIGURE HOLDING THE REINS...!

A MAN WITHOUT A FACE!
THE GHOST RIDER!

GET AWAY! GET AWAY!
DEATH IS MY BUSINESS, FACELESS ONE! I RIDE THE NIGHT WINDS SEEKING EVIL AND STAMPING IT OUT... AND SOMETHING TELLS ME YOU ARE EVIL ITSELF!

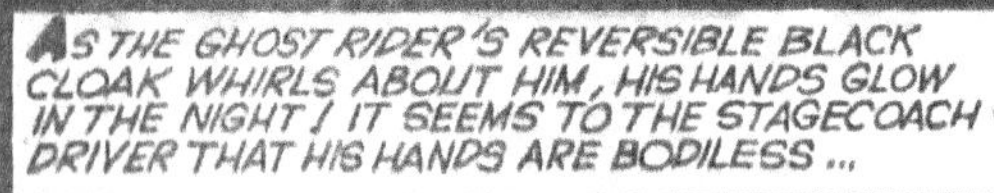
AS THE GHOST RIDER'S REVERSIBLE BLACK CLOAK WHIRLS ABOUT HIM, HIS HANDS GLOW IN THE NIGHT! IT SEEMS TO THE STAGECOACH DRIVER THAT HIS HANDS ARE BODILESS ...

AAAGGHH!

IT IS TIME FOR VILLAINY TO UNMASK!

AT THAT MOMENT, ONE OF THE WHEELS STRIKES A LARGE ROCK, THE STAGECOACH BOUNCES VIOLENTLY, SWERVES SHARPLY, AND...
LOST MY FOOTING! GOING TO TAKE A SPILL ...!
ALMOST... CHOKED ME TO DEATH! ¡GASP!

COVERED BY HIS GREAT BLACK CLOAK, THE GHOST RIDER LIES ALMOST INVISIBLE ON THE GROUND...
¡GULP! HE'S GONE! DISAPPEARED!
4

AS DAWN TINTS THE NEARBY HILLS NEXT MORNING, A PALEFACED MAN STARES DOWN AT A SKULL —
A SKULL! AND—AND THIS ONE HAS MY NAME ON IT! I'LL BE KILLED... SAME AS LUKE AND JEB WERE KILLED!

TOM— LOOK! ONE OF THOSE INFERNAL SKULLS! I'M THE NEXT TO GO!
EASY, ROGER! I WANT TO INTRODUCE YOU TO REX FURY, A U.S. MARSHAL!
ROGER BOOFER

IT'S EASY ENOUGH TO FIGURE OUT. SOMEBODY AIMS TO GET RID OF THE FOUR MOST IMPORTANT MEN IN CACTUS GAP. WHY? PERHAPS THE KILLER INTENDS TO TAKE OVER YOUR PROPERTY... EVENTUALLY!
NONSENSE! THERE'S NOBODY 'ROUND THESE PARTS ABLE TO DO THAT—— UNLESS—

UNLESS IT'S ONE OF US! THAT MEANS YOU'RE THE ONE, TOM! YOU COLD-BLOODED MURDERER!
HOLD ON, NOW! I'M NOT THE MAN! ROGER— YOU'RE PLUMB LOCO! MAYBE YOU'RE THE ONE YOURSELF!

EASY, EASY! WE WON'T GET ANYWHERE THROWING ACCUSATIONS AROUND. BREAK IT UP, NOW! WE'LL WAIT FOR FURTHER DEVELOPMENTS!
THAT'S ALL RIGHT FOR YOU. NOBODY'S THREATENING YOUR LIFE!
I SAY— WAIT!

THAT NIGHT, AS ROGER BOOFER RIDES HOME ALONE —

SUDDENLY THE GROUND ERUPTS UNDER HIM! BITS OF FLYING ROCK FLY THROUGH THE AIR!
THE WHOLE SIDE OF THE CLIFF CAVED IN!

I HEARD AN EXPLOSION! ARE YOU ALL RIGHT?
I THINK SO.! IT WAS SO SUDDEN, I JUST HAD TIME TO KICK MY FEET OUT OF THE STIRRUPS AND HOP FREE ... YEOW! THE GHOST RIDER!

HMMM.! SOMETHING MIGHTY ODD ABOUT THIS.! THAT EXPLOSION WAS SO POWERFUL, IT KNOCKED HIS HORSE OVER THE EDGE OF THE CLIFF — AND YET BOOFER IS UNMARKED BY BURNS — NOT EVEN SCRATCHED.!

LATER THAT NIGHT, AS ROGER BOOFER PREPARES FOR BED...
ROGER BOOFER! CAN YOU SLEEP NIGHTS? DO NOT THE DEATHS OF LUKE MORMON AND JEB NOLAN HAUNT YOUR DREAMS?
3 GASP!

YOU'RE MAD! I-I DON'T KNOW WHY YOU FOLLOWED ME — BUT I'M INNOCENT!
ARE YOU, ROGER BOOFER? DID YOU NOT PLAN THAT DYNAMITE TRAP TO THROW SUSPICION OFF YOURSELF? CLEVER.! BUT NOT CLEVER ENOUGH. REMEMBER — THE GHOST RIDER KNOWS!

HE — HE'S GONE! DISAPPEARED.! 3 GULP! HE ISN'T HUMAN! BUT HE CAN'T BLUFF ME.! I'M NOT SCARED OF HIM! I'VE PLANNED ALL THIS TOO CAREFULLY TO MAKE A MISTAKE NOW!

BEING AN OLD FRIEND OF MORMON, NOLAN AND BRENNAN, I'LL INHERIT PART OF THEIR LAND AND CATTLE.! WE ALL MADE WILLS AT THE SAME TIME, IN THE SAME WAY. WITH THAT ADDED LAND AND CATTLE, I'LL BE ABLE TO BUY OUT THEIR WIDOWS! I'LL GET TO BE A POWER IN THE STATE — EVENTUALLY GET TO CONGRESS.!

THE GHOST RIDER HAS NO PROOF! — NOTHING THAT WILL STAND UP IN COURT.! ONE MORE RIDE IN MY SPECTRAL STAGECOACH, AND WHEN TOM BRENNAN DIES — I'VE WON!

ONCE AGAIN THE WHEELS OF THE STAGECOACH OF DEATH RATTLE AND BOUNCE! ONCE AGAIN THE FACELESS COWLED DRIVER HOLDS THE REINS...
OUR LAST RIDE, MY BEAUTIES! TONIGHT WE TRAVEL DEATH'S HIGHWAY FOR THE LAST TIME! RUN! RUN!

SUDDENLY, SUSPENDED IN THE AIR ITSELF —!
YOU WHO RIDE ON DEATH'S BUSINESS... — GREETINGS!

YOU!
THIS TIME THERE IS NO ESCAPE, MY FRIEND!

THIS TIME, WHEN I FALL OFF THE COACH, YOU WILL FALL WITH ME!
NO! NO!

ROGER BOOFER! I KNEW IT! YOU KILLED LUKE MORMON ... AND POISONED JEB NOLAN SO THAT HE DIED IN THE SAGE FLATS! YOU SERVED DEATH WELL! BUT YOU WILL SERVE HIM EVEN BETTER —

— WHEN THEY HANG YOU FOR YOUR CRIMES!

OUR JOB IS DONE! ONCE AGAIN THE EVIL THAT STALKS BY NIGHT HAS FADED OUT! UP SPECTRE! AWAY!

"SINCE IT IS SO LIKELY THAT (CHILDREN) WILL MEET CRUEL ENEMIES, LET THEM AT LEAST HAVE HEARD OF BRAVE KNIGHTS AND HEROIC COURAGE. OTHERWISE YOU ARE MAKING THEIR DESTINY NOT BRIGHTER BUT DARKER."

— C.S. LEWIS

"FAIRY TALES DO NOT TELL CHILDREN THE DRAGONS EXIST. CHILDREN ALREADY KNOW THAT DRAGONS EXIST. FAIRY TALES TELL CHILDREN THE DRAGONS CAN BE KILLED."

— G.K. CHESTERTON

LEGENDARIUM

BY MICHAEL BUNKER & KEVIN G. SUMMERS

CHAPTER THREE
BEYOND THE STARS

They emerged, through an airlock, into what could only be a science fiction story. They knew it was an airlock because the words "AIRLOCK 03" were stenciled in black paint above the door that swished closed behind them. And they knew it was a science fiction story because of the airlock. And the rivets. There were rivets everywhere. *Everywhere.* Because in the future, apparently everything is riveted together just like it was in the 1940's.

"Where in the multiverse have we landed this time? Bombo said.

Alistair's eyebrows furrowed as he scanned the room. "This seems familiar," he said, "but I can't quite place it."

Before they could consider the matter further, another door swished open on the opposite side of the airlock. A man in a pair of dark blue coveralls stepped through the door. He had a round face and a large, pointed nose. A lit cigarette hung from the corner of his mouth. The name HENRY was embroidered over his heart—though whether this was his first name or his last, neither Bombo nor Alistair could say—and he had rank insignia on his collar.

"Ensign Foley," he said. "Did you recover the borogoves?"

Bombo and Alistair looked at one another in confusion. "Borogoves?"

"Sonofabitch!" said Henry. "We sent you down to that planet to collect some borogoves. You know that's the only thing that can save the captain."

"Borogoves?" Alistair asked again.

"Borogoves!" Henry repeated angrily.

"Oh!" Bombo said, as if struck by a sudden understanding. "Borogoves!" He looked at Alistair and nodded. He didn't have the slightest clue what anyone was talking about, but he liked to keep the conversation moving.

Then Alistair gasped. He knew this story. He had no time to process this knowledge, however, because Henry shoved past Bombo and grabbed Alistair by the shoulders. "You knew that the captain's life was in your hands, Ensign Foley! Why the hell did you come back without the borogoves?"

"Um, sorry," Alistair said.

Bombo snickered. "Ensign Foley," he repeated.

Henry took his hands off of Alistair and stepped back a half-step. He took a drag on his cigarette and then dropped it to the deck at their feet. He stamped it out with the toe of his boot. "It doesn't matter now," he said. "The Martians are on their way to the station with an armada. We're all going to be dead in a few minutes." He paused for a breath, then added: "Thanks to you two."

Shaking his head in frustration, Henry turned and headed back through the swishy door through which he'd entered. He disappeared into a sterile corridor, leaving Bombo and Alistair alone inside the airlock.

Bombo turned to Alistair and was amazed to see that his nemesis was now wearing blue coveralls that matched Henry's. The name FOLEY was embroidered over his heart. Bombo looked down at himself and saw that he was also wearing a matching uniform.

"What *is* this place?" he asked. "Oh, and I *love* uniforms!"

"The space station Alamo 02," Alistair said. "You love uniforms?"

"Not really," Bombo said. "I was being ironical."

"Actually you were being sarcastic," Alistair said. "And if I'm not mistaken, this is *The Last Outpost*, the final novel in the *Beyond the Stars* series."

"*Beyond the Stars?*" Bombo said. He nodded his head and then stopped and shook it vigorously. "I tried to read the first one. I couldn't get past the second chapter."

"You have really terrible taste in books," Alistair said. "No surprise given how poorly you write."

"You're a real pleasure to be around, Foley," said Bombo. "Has anyone ever told you that?"

"*Beyond the Stars* is one of the most important works of science fiction ever written, and Russell Benjamin's magnum opus. Do you know how many young African-Americans were inspired by the story? Martin Luther King mentioned Benjamin by name in his inaugural address."

"I know, I know," Bombo said, "But just because President King liked a book doesn't mean that *I* have to. And just because I didn't like it, doesn't mean that I don't know and appreciate the history of it. Benjamin wrote about a black man commanding a space station in a time when black men weren't allowed to drink from white water fountains. But the story itself is so dated. You saw that character with the cigarette…"

"You've been complaining about wanting a cigar for hours," Alistair said.

"That's different," said Bombo. "Cigarettes are bad for you."

Alistair just stared at the big man for a few seconds. At last, he decided not to grapple with Dawson on this point. Some fights you have to leave for a more opportune time.

"Anyway, we have a major problem here," Alistair said.

"Why's that?"

"That character who just spoke to us was Doctor James Henry," Alistair said. "In the novel, he sent an away team on a mission to recover some plants that he used to save the life of the station's commander."

"So what's the problem?"

"We didn't recover the borogoves," Alistair said. "Without them, Captain Haley is going to die, and the Martians are going to destroy this station."

As if to emphasize this point, an alarm klaxon began to sound all over the station. A voice crackled from a speaker overhead: "All hands to battle stations. Lieutenant Dawson, report to Ops. Ensign Foley, report to the Infirmary."

"How is the story *supposed* to end?" Bombo asked.

"Doctor Henry revives the captain just in time," Alistair said. "And he uses his cunning to defeat the Martian armada."

"And what do you think will happen if the ending changes?"

"The story will collapse, we'll die, and the history of the past sixty years will be altered in our own world," Alistair said.

Bombo sighed. "Of all the novels in the world, this is literally the last one in which I'd want to find myself."

"What about *A Game Of Thrones?*"

Bombo thought for a moment. "Well, you got me there. I think that would be even worse."

"You're serious? Everyone likes *A Game Of Thrones*."

"No," Bombo said, "not everyone. I don't like it. And believe me, I tried. They march around for two hundred and fifty pages, then someone gets murdered and someone gets raped or something. Then they march around for another two hundred and fifty pages talking about some place they never seem to be actually going. Then someone gets murdered or raped or both, and then the book ends and they never even got close to going to the mythical place they were all talking about."

Alistair shook his head in disbelief. "What about *The Crystal Shard*?"

"Could I meet some elves? That would be just peachy."

"*You* are the reason that everyone hates Americans," Alistair said. "You, you, you!"

"What can I say? Fantasy sucks, and so does space opera."

"Well, we're here," Alistair said, "so get over it."

"Do you think it was a good idea for Benjamin to name this space station after the Alamo?" Bombo asked.

Now it was Alistair's turn to sigh. "It was foreshadowing."

Bombo nodded. "I hate it when I'm in a story and there's foreshadowing of doom."

Bombo arrived in the *Alamo-02* Operations Center after a hearty jog through the corridors of the space station. He was winded from the exercise, and desperately craving a cigar and a donut, and maybe a cup of black coffee. If he was going to die, he wanted to do it in comfort. *They probably didn't have donuts at the original Alamo either*, he thought.

"Lieutenant Dawson," said a man with slicked-back hair and a set of overlarge sideburns, "so glad you could join us."

"Yes, sir," Bombo said. He stared awkwardly at the man and then saluted him, because it seemed liked the right thing to do. The name embroidered on the man's coveralls was STUYVESANT. An insignia on his collar indicated that he held the rank of commander.

"Take your post," Commander Stuyvesant ordered. "The Martians will be here any minute."

Bombo took a look around Ops. There were rolling office chairs parked in front of archaic computer terminals. What appeared to be an old-fashioned television loomed over the room; it must have been three feet wide and was nearly as thick. There was a dedication plaque mounted on one wall, and beneath it, a sword wrapped in an American flag and clutched in the claws of a screaming eagle. Apparently the Good ol' US of A was alive and well in this futuristic world.

"Excuse me, sir," Bombo said. "Could you please tell me which post is mine?"

Commander Stuyvesant glared at him. "Were you injured on your away mission?" he said.

"No, sir."

"And the reason you didn't return with the medicine that could have saved the captain…?"

Bombo shuffled in place. "We… um… we forgot."

"You forgot," Stuyvesant said. Scorn dripped from his words. "Now the captain is going to die because of your stupidity."

"We could go back…" Bombo said. He indicated with his thumb back over his shoulder.

"And not just the captain—everyone else on this ship too," Stuyvesant added.

"…back through the swishy door to get the borogoves," Bombo said.

"There's no time for that," said Stuyvesant. As if to emphasize the point, another officer interrupted their conversation.

"Commander," he said, "we are receiving an incoming transmission from the Martians."

"Put it on the monitor," said the commander.

The television set flickered to life, and Bombo saw, to his surprise, a living shadow staring back at him. It made a terrible, high-pitched sound that rang throughout Ops. Everyone covered their ears. Behind the creature, other living shadows boiled and shifted in the background.

"Oh my," Bombo said. "The Martians are Mome Wraiths."

When the doors slid open onto the infirmary, Alistair saw the captain of the *Alamo-02* lying on his deathbed. Doctor Henry was standing over his commanding officer, the first negro to ever command a space station. The word *negro*, of course, belonged to Russell Benjamin, the author of this story. It was common usage at the time, but Alistair was nevertheless surprised when it appeared as part of his mental vocabulary.

Doctor Henry looked up as Alistair entered the room. "You," he snapped. "Get over here."

Ensign Foley scurried across the room. The captain's eyes were closed tight, his breathing labored. His close-cropped hair glistened with sweat.

"You let him down," said the doctor. "You let us *all* down, and I want you to watch as your commander breathes his last."

"Is that truly necessary?" Alistair said. "I feel really bad about—"

"Ensign," came the strained voice of the captain. "Come close. I want… I need… to tell you…"

Alistair leaned over the captain. He looked just like Russell Benjamin. "Sir," he whispered. "I'm truly sorry…"

"Listen," the captain said. "Don't lose sight of your mission."

"To defend the station?" said Alistair.

"No," said the captain. His breathing was strained, and he seemed to be speaking purely by force of will. "This station is called the *Alamo-02*, son. You should have picked up on that."

Alistair wanted to say "I did," but he didn't have the heart.

"Yes, sir," was all he said.

"No. You must find the sword," the captain whispered.

"Sir?"

"This world is dying," said the captain. "You can't save it now. You must get the sword." He closed his eyes, took a deep breath, and then exhaled slowly. He did not take another.

Doctor Henry bowed his head. "He's dead."

"Jim?" said a nurse in a tight-fitting uniform. Her hair was stacked and curled and swooshed in a manner that was unmistakably fifties. She gave Alistair a disgusted look and then turned her back on him.

As Doctor Henry and his nurse discussed something privately, Alistair made his way over to a computer terminal. The machine was archaic; it hummed and clicked and was covered all over with inexplicable switches and dials. There was a chrome-plated microphone bolted to it, and since he saw no keyboard or monitor, Alistair assumed that this was how he was supposed to interface with the machine.

"Computer," he said. "Search the term *borogove*."

The computer whistled and rattled and chugged, and a moment later a slip of paper rolled out of a slit in the machine. Dot matrix words were printed on the paper. They read:

1 reference for the term "borogove" was found. Term is a nonsense word from Lewis Carroll's poem "Jabberwocky" which appeared in Through The Looking Glass and What Alice Found There.

Reference:
'Twas brillig, and the
slithy toves
Did gyre and gimble in
the wabe;
All mimsy were the
borogoves,
And the mome raths
outgrabe.

"Lewis freakin' Carroll," Alistair said. "That son of a—"

"What are you doing?" It was the stern voice of Doctor Henry.

"Oh, um, I'm sorry. I was researching—"

"The captain is dead, the station is about to be invaded by Martians, and you're wasting time on the computer? Whose side are you on, son?"

Foley averted his eyes. Was there some way of saving this story? "I'm sorry, sir," he said. "Is there anything I can do?"

"Ensign," said the doctor, "I think you've done quite enough already."

Just then, the space station's loud-speakers crackled to life, and Bombo's voice boomed. "Ensign Foley, please report to Ops on the double."

WHEN ALISTAIR STEPPED INTO THE OPER-ations Center, the first thing he noticed was the terrible look on Bombo's face. Not that Bombo was ever much to look at, what with that ridiculous beard and all, but now he looked downright ill.

"Bombo?" Alistair said. "What's wrong?"

Bombo moved closer to Alistair so that he wouldn't be overheard. "The Martians," he said. "I saw them on the monitor."

"And?"

"They're Mome Wraiths, just like the ones we saw in Wonderland."

"Mome Wraiths?" Alistair said. "That's odd."

Bombo fidgeted with his beard. "You bet your bippy it's odd."

"Do you have any idea where we might look for the sword?" Alistair asked.

"None whatsoever," Bombo said. "And in about five minutes, this station is going to be overrun with evil shadow monster thingies."

"I accessed their computer," Alistair said. "Borogoves are some kind of plant from Lewis Carroll's Jabberwocky poem. At least, I think it's a plant. It's hard to tell with him."

"I know that poem," Bombo said. He thought for a minute. "Doesn't it say something about Mome Wraiths?"

Alistair took another look at the printout. "It says *mome raths*," he said. "Maybe Lewis Carroll somehow predicted the coming of the shadows, but he got the name wrong. Like Nostradamus when he talked about an evil tyrant named Hister."

"Maybe it's just a nonsense word," said Bombo. "Sometimes a hat is just a hat."

"And sometimes it's a symbol of the underlying theme of the story. Did you ever think of that?"

Before Bombo could answer, a barrage of enemy fire shook the space station.

"Return fire!" shouted Commander Stuyvesant.

A weapons officer flipped some switches and turned some dials on the massive mainframe that dominated one corner of the room. "Direct hit," he said. "We've destroyed their lead ship."

"How many does that leave?" Stuyvesant asked.

"Two hundred ninety-nine," said the weapons officer.

"We're doomed," said the commander. "If only Captain Haley were here."

"No," Alistair said loudly. "We have to fight. I know a way to defeat the Martians."

The station shook as Martian fire bombarded their shields. "Shields down to fifty-two percent," said the weapons officer.

"Fire at will!" shouted Stuyvesant.

"What are you doing?" Bombo said.

"I've read this book a dozen times," Alistair said. "I know how Captain Haley bested the Martians."

Commander Stuyvesant took a cautious step toward Alistair. "Ensign," he said, "were you part of the mission to retrieve a plant that could have saved the captain?"

"Yes, sir," Alistair said.

Stuyvesant scowled. "That mission was a failure!" He pointed a bony finger at Alistair. "So what makes you think I'm going to trust you with the fate of every member of this crew?"

"Because you have no choice, sir," Alistair said. "I know a way that we can defeat the Martians, and unless I'm mistaken, you're out of ideas."

Another barrage of enemy fire rocked the station. "Shields are down to nineteen percent," said the weapons officer.

Though he was nearly thrown off his feet, Stuyvesant steadied himself and glared at Alistair. "I do not like you, Ensign Foley."

"Welcome to the team, sir," Bombo said.

Stuyvesant looked from Alistair to Bombo. "You worked with this man, Lieutenant. Should I trust him?"

For Bombo, giving an endorsement of Alistair Foley was about the hardest thing he ever had to do—except maybe for trying to stay on Carol's diet—but this was a matter of life and death. He swallowed his own dislike of Ensign Foley and nodded his head. "He's an excellent officer, sir. I think you should trust him."

Stuyvesant nodded his head thoughtfully as the station shook once again. "Fine," he said. "What's your plan, Ensign?"

"If you adjust the station's shield harmonics," Alistair said, "to match the harmonics of the Martian's shields, and then calibrate our deflector dish to generate a reverse resonance burst—"

Before he could finish explaining his elaborate plan, Alistair was cut off by the weapons officer. "Shields have collapsed," he said. "And the deflector dish has been destroyed."

"Well, so much for that," Bombo said. "It was a good plan for the five seconds it was under consideration."

Alistair stared at Bombo in shock. "That's how Captain Haley did it in the book," he said. "Now I don't know what to do."

"We're being boarded!" Stuyvesant shouted. "All hands, abandon ship!"

"Abandon ship?" Bombo said. "That's an odd phrase to use in the inky blackness and oxygen-less void of space."

Mome Wraiths began to materialize all over Ops. The weapons officer stood and shot one with a laser pistol. The shadow exploded with a shriek, but it was too little, too late. A swarm of Mome Wraiths converged on the officer, stretching their claw-like hands toward the doomed man. His frightful screams tore through the room as the shadows enveloped him. Within a few seconds, he had become a Mome Wraith, screeching like all the others and slithering toward Bombo and Alistair.

"Come on," Bombo said. "Time to get out of here." He grabbed Alistair and dragged him toward a swishy door. Above the door were stenciled the words *Escape Pod*. The door swished open and they barely made it inside before a host of Mome Wraiths swarmed them. One creature reached its shadowy hand into the pod just before the door swished closed, severing the Mome Wraith's hand. It lay twitching on the floor for several seconds before it melted into nothing and disappeared.

The escape pod had a small round window that allowed the two writers a momentary view of the raging battle for the Operations Center. Stuyvesant, brave and heedless of the danger, was still fighting, shooting Mome Wraiths and narrowly dodging the reaching hands of other shadows, but it was only a matter of time. In the seconds before the escape pod launched, Bombo and Alistair watched in horror as Stuyvesant's laser pistol failed.

Weaponless, the first officer dodged one Mome Wraith, leapt over a railing, and grabbed the ceremonial sword that was mounted to the wall. Stuyvesant unwrapped the American flag from the blade and draped it over his shoulder, never letting it touch the ground. The sword gleamed under the fluorescent lights of the space station as Stuyvesant used it to chop an approaching Mome Wraith in half.

At that moment, the escape pod's thrusters fired and Bombo and Alistair were propelled into space. The *Alamo-02* receded in the distance, and the battle that raged inside receded too.

Bombo and Alistair turned to one another. "Did you see that?" Bombo said. "He must have had some kind of fencing training. That was awesome."

"We're idiots," Alistair said. "That was the vorpal sword."

Bombo stared at Alistair. "The ceremonial sword that was on the wall?"

"The vorpal sword," Alistair said.

"That's quite a leap," said Bombo. "Why would the vorpal sword be on the space station? It doesn't even belong in this story."

"Neither do the Mome Wraiths or borogoves," Alistair said. "The worlds of the Legendarium are bleeding together."

"This is exhausting," Bombo said. "I could really use a donut."

"We have to get back to the station," said Alistair. "We have to recover the—"

Before he could finish, the space station *Alamo-02* exploded. Orange light flashed across the faces of the two men as they realized that their mission had failed. Stars began to wink out all around them, and their escape pod drifted through a darkening void as the evil living shadows engulfed the universe.

CHAPTER FOUR
THE FACE OF THE DEEP

THEY DRIFTED THROUGH THE VOID.

★ ★ ★

BACK IN THE REAL WORLD, IN THE WORLD where you are reading this story, a tsunami of changes crashed over the space-time continuum.

Martin Luther King, who should have been inspired by Russell Benjamin's *Beyond the Stars* series as a young man, had now never read it—and so was never elected as the fortieth president of the United States. Instead, he was assassinated in Memphis, Tennessee on April 4, 1968.

The peace treaty between Israel and Iran moderated by Jimmy Carter in 1988 was never signed.

Russell Benjamin, instead of being the first African-American to win both the Nebula and Hugo awards, went mad in 1953 and was committed to a sanitarium for the rest of his life.

A hundred thousand other changes rippled up and down the timeline. Life for some; death for others. Dreams fulfilled; dreams shattered. The changes were systemic, and you'll never know what the original world was really like. Sorry.

★ ★ ★

THEY DRIFTED FOR WHAT SEEMED LIKE AN eternity, and in truth, millennia did pass unnumbered as Bombo Dawson and Alistair Foley floated through the darkness.

They talked because there was nothing else to do.

"These emergency rations are running low," Alistair said. It was perhaps five days into their odyssey. It was also, perhaps, five hundred years. If time is meaningless in the Legendarium, it is both tedious and confusing in an escape pod with Alistair Foley and Bombo Dawson.

"I wish there were donuts," Bombo said. "I'd do anything for a donut."

"You ate all the freeze-dried ice cream," Alistair said. "You could have at least saved me one package."

"I'm starving to death," Bombo said. "I'm wasting away to nothing. Look at me. My space coveralls are just hanging on my gaunt and emaciated frame. This is an emergency."

"You haven't even lost a pound, Bombo. We're floating through the emptiness of a ruined universe. Alone. In an escape pod. Together alone, Bombo. This is my own personal hell."

"And yet, I'm probably starving, which is the real issue at hand," Bombo replied.

"If you die," Alistair said, "I'm going to eat you. I want you to remember that."

"There won't be anything left to eat," said Bombo.

Alistair rubbed his temples. His head had been throbbing for hours, or centuries, or millennia. "Of all the people to be stuck with… lost in the vacuum of space… why did it have to be you?"

"You're not exactly pleasant company yourself," Bombo said. "I wish there was something here to read."

"I have an e-reader on my smart phone," Alistair said, "but the battery died back in Wonderland. "It kept searching for signal."

"I highly doubt that there is anything on your Kindle that I would want to read," Bombo said.

"That's probably true," said Alistair. "I doubt your taste in literature is that refined."

"Please," said Bombo. "My taste in books is way better than yours."

"You don't like Russell Benjamin," Alistair said.

"And you don't like Lewis Carroll," said Bombo.

They stared at one another, mentally drawing up sides in the contest of one-upmanship that was about to follow.

"What about Tolkien?" Alistair said.

"He's okay," said Bombo. "I don't like fantasy. I thought we covered that."

"Margaret Weis and Tracy Hickman?" Alistair asked.

"You're joking, right?"

"Stephen King?"

"Hate him, although his time travel book about the Kennedy assassination was at least interesting."

"J.K. Rowling?"

Bombo stuck his index finger in his mouth and mimed throwing up.

"Vonnegut?"

"Love him."

"Well, that's a relief. Salvatore?"

"Who?"

"R.A. Salvatore."

Bombo chuckled under his breath.

"Dayton Ward? Kevin Dilmore?

"They write *Star Trek* novels," Bombo said.

"Right. Do you like them?"

"They write *Star Trek* novels," Bombo said again.

"Moron," Alistair whispered.

"What was that?"

"Nothing. How about James A. Owen?"

"Um."

"Hugh Howey?"

Bombo smiled. He knew Hugh Howey personally. Together, they had saved London, and perhaps the entire world, from a zombie apocalypse. "I love his work," Bombo said.

Alistair nodded enthusiastically. "Me too. I didn't want to like *the COTTON Omnibus*, it being self-published and all, but after I read it, I had to admit that it was brilliant."

"What's wrong with self-publishing?" Bombo asked.

"There's so much potential for crap," Alistair said.

Bombo shrugged. "Same with legacy publishing. The cream rises to the top," Bombo said.

"I suppose that's true," Alistair said.

"When was the last time you were in a bookstore, Alistair?"

"I go to bookstores all the time."

"How would you rate most of the books in the last book store you visited?"

"A tsunami of crap," Alistair said, nodding his head. "But the cream rises to the top."

"And probably none of them were self-published," Bombo said. "There's crap everywhere, but still we find what we want to read. You know, we have dozens of tools that we use every day to decide what we might like. The indie world is no different."

"I suppose you're right," Alistair said.

"Since we're apparently going to drift through this empty universe until we starve to death," Bombo said, "would you mind answering a question?"

"Go for it."

"What was it about *Anne Askew in the Tower* that you hated so much that you decided to give it such a terrible review? I mean, your opinion was not remotely in line with the vast majority of readers of every possible stripe. I mean, everyone has their own opinion, but really: one star?"

Alistair paused thoughtfully. He had never before come face to face with the victim of one of his scathing reviews. "I think it was the stream of consciousness," he said. "I really don't care for that style."

"I can dig that," Bombo said, "Did you like the characters? The plot?"

"Those were fine," Alistair said. "Truthfully, the book wasn't that bad. It's just…"

"Just what?"

Alistair averted his eyes, unable to look Bombo in the face. "I guess I was jealous," he said.

"Jealous? Of what?"

Alistair gazed through the escape pod's portal into the abyss. The abyss also gazed into him. "Do you remember when Thornton Wilder said that he'd read my book?"

"Yeah."

"I've been sending it out to literary agents for three years," Alistair said. "I have a pile of personal rejection letters, each one telling me how much they love my book and that they wish me well finding someone to represent it."

"That sucks," Bombo said. "But what agents want and what readers want are often very different things. Publishing has gotten top-heavy. In many cases it isn't agile enough to track with what readers want to buy. Have you ever considered self-publishing?"

"No," Alistair said. "I mean, yes. I mean, I've thought about it, but who would ever read it? How would I market the book?"

"Indie publishing really isn't about trying to make a book a bestseller, Alistair. It's about the art of writing. It's about finishing the work and making it as good as it can possibly be. Then it's about publishing it and letting *readers* decide if they want to buy it. Besides, Hugh Howey is just one of hundreds of other successful authors that have done all right with self-publishing," Bombo said.

"That's different," Alistair said. "He's an outlier."

"Thornton Wilder and Leo Tolstoy seemed to like your writing," Bombo said. "What are the chances that *War and Peace* would ever be published by a mainstream publisher today? Close to zero? But two of the greatest authors in history liked your work! That should be an encouragement to you."

Alistair smiled slightly. "Yeah. Maybe you're right."

"I mean, I'm absolutely going to give it one star no matter whether I like it or not," Bombo said, "because you've been such a tool—but maybe it could find an audience. Stuck in a drawer somewhere… it *never* will. And you'll never know unless you try."

Alistair sighed. "I guess I owe you an apology," he said. "That review was pretty crummy of me."

"You can say that again," Bombo said.

"Maybe I should revise it," Alistair said. "If we ever get back."

"I don't think there's much chance of that happening," Bombo said. "Besides, I don't think anyone reads your blog."

"Has anyone ever told you that you're an asshat?" Alistair said.

"Lots of folks," Bombo said. "My wife tells me at least once a week."

"You're married?"

"Why do you sound so surprised?"

Alistair stared out the porthole into the nothingness of the void. "I don't know. It seems like everybody has somebody except me."

"You sound like a country and western song," Bombo said.

Alistair growled. "I hate country music."

"Shocker."

"Are you happily married?"

"Yep."

"Your wife isn't a psycho or something?"

"She's a communist and a vegetarian, although she denies that first thing… just like a good communist would do."

"Oh," Alistair said. "Well, that makes me feel a little better."

"But she's smoking hot, and I know she loves me."

"How do you know?"

"Have you *seen* me?"

"You have a point. She loves you." Alistair sighed a deep, pathetic, look-at-me kind of sigh. "I had a girlfriend up until about two months ago," he said.

"She dumped you?"

"How did you guess?"

Bombo shrugged. "A hunch."

"She was… so… beautiful." Alistair wiped at his eyes.

"Hey man, there's other fish in the sea."

"I don't know," Alistair said. "I think I'm done with women."

Bombo backed away from Alistair, creating as much space as humanly possible in the tiny escape pod. "Cut off that stupid ponytail," he suggested. "I'm sure there's someone out there who could tolerate you. Have you tried online dating?"

"You're such a—"

The small craft was rocked by a violent jolt, and both writers were thrown across the escape pod. They landed in a pile, arms and legs akimbo, as their transport crash-landed onto something solid. When the pod had skidded to a stop, a deafening silence settled over the pod as Bombo and Alistair just looked at one another, wide-eyed and not at all sure what might happen next.

Wherever here is, Bombo thought, *here we are.*

FIRE AND ICE

Some say the world will end in fire,
    Some say in ice.
From what I've tasted of desire
I hold with those who favor fire.
    But if it had to perish twice,
I think I know enough of hate
    To know that for destruction ice
Is also great,
    And would suffice.

— Robert Frost, 1922

LINDA TURNER, HOLLYWOOD STAR AND AMERICA'S SWEETHEART, BECOMES BORED WITH HER ULTRA-SOPHISTICATED LIFE OF MOVIE MAKE-BELIEVE AND TAKES TO CRIME-FIGHTING IN HER MOST DRAMATIC ROLE OF ALL AS THE ----
BLACK CAT
HOLLYWOOD'S GLAMOROUS DETECTIVE STAR
Who is the BLACK CAT?
LINDA TURNER, GLAMOUROUS MOVIE QUEEN, DOES A DOUBLE TAKE WHEN..
RICK HORNE, HOLLYWOOD GOSSIP MAN, SPRINGS THE BLACK CAT CONTEST AND JOINS FORCES WITH...
THE ROOK, CHESS EXPERT, DETERMINED TO EXTERMINATE THE BLACK CAT! BUT FIRST HE MUST ANSWER THIS QUESTION, TOO ----
Who is the BLACK CAT?
LEE ELIAS

YEAH? SO WHAT, ROOK? SO BLACK CAT TRIES TO BREAK UP OUR RACKETS? WHAT CAN YOU DO?
SURE! YOU AN' YER BIG IDEAS!
SILENCE! I MAKE THE DECISIONS! NOT YOU STUPID SHYSTERS! BLACK CAT MUST BE EXTERMINATED AT ONCE! SHALL I TELL YOU WHY?

"REMEMBER KNUCKLES MORGAN? HE AND HIS MEN OPERATED A REALLY SLICK BANK BUSTING SCHEME TILL SHE APPEARED, AND--"

"SUBSEQUENTLY KNUCKLES AND CO. WERE SENTENCED TO FORTY YEARS! ALL BECAUSE OF BLACK CAT!"

"AND REMEMBER THE JONES BOYS? THEY WERE KING PINS OF CRIME LAST YEAR TILL ONE NIGHT THAT BLACK CAT--"

"PUT HER TWO CENTS INTO ONE OF THEIR CLEVER TRAIN ROBBERIES AND THAT WAS THE END OF THE JONES BOYS!"

MUST I GO ON? OR DO YOU ALL UNDERSTAND WHY WE MUST FORM AN UNDERWORLD CHAMBER OF COMMERCE WHICH ORGANIZATION'S PURPOSE SHALL BE TO ERASE ALL ANTI-CRIME FORCES ARRAYED AGAINST US--ESPECIALLY BLACK CAT!
YEAH? WE PAY DUES TO YA, EH? AN' I SUPPOSE Y'NOMINATE YERSELF TO BE PRESIDENT, EH?

NATURALLY--PAWN--JUMP THAT KNAVE!!
I'M WISE TA YUH! I'LL--YAAAAAGOHH...!

YOUR ATTENTION, SCUM! NOW LISTEN CLOSELY--FOR OUR NEXT--(HA-HA) MOVE!

DAYS LATER, BILLBOARDS BLANKET THE NATION--
STUPENDOUS! COLOSSAL! TITANIC!
WIN $50,000.00
BY IDENTIFYING THE BLACK CAT! WHO IS SHE? TELL AND WIN! MAIL ALL ENTRIES TO:
P.O. Box 13

A NATION WITH BUT ONE THOUGHT--WHO IS BLACK CAT?

--AND ENTRIES POUR THROUGH THE MAILS--THE FRENZY OF MILLIONS GONE CONTEST CRAZY--BUT DOES ONE ENTRY BLANK BEAR THE VITAL ANSWER?!--

BLACK CAT CONTEST! HMM-- SOMEONE IS VERY CURIOUS AND CURIOSITY KILLED A CAT--BUT THE BLACK CAT--
BLACK CAT CONTEST BECOMES NATIONAL RAGE!
--HAS NINE LIVES!
WHILE IN HOLLYWOOD'S RADIO CITY, RICK HORNE, FAMED GOSSIP REPORTER, REHEARSES HIS PROGRAM--
GOOD EVENING! ONCE AGAIN IT'S GOSSIP TIME IN HOLLYWOOD! AT CIRO'S LAST NIGHT--
PARDON, MR. HORNE--IT'S THE CHESS EXPERT, MR. ROOK TO SEE YOU--
THE ROOK HIMSELF! SEND HIM RIGHT IN!
--AND CONFIDENTIALLY SPEAKING, I'M RUNNING THIS BLACK CAT CONTEST-- HOW ABOUT GIVING IT SOME REAL PUBLICITY IN YOUR BROADCAST-- IT'LL BE THE TALK OF THE TOWN!
SAY THAT'S A SWELL IDEA! I'LL CHANGE MY SCRIPT RIGHT NOW! GREAT STUNT, ROOK!
HERE'S A TERRIFIC ITEM! GET IN ON THE SENSATIONAL BIG MONEY! ENTER THE CONTEST ON "WHO IS BLACK CAT"--DO YOU KNOW?

WHILE ACROSS BEVERLY HILLS, IN GLAMOUR GAL LINDA TURNER'S DRESSING ROOM--
AWWRRK--AND--IF YOU THINK YOU KNOW WHO SHE REALLY IS, SEND YOUR GUESS TO POST OFFICE BOX--
SOME FUN! SO NOW RICK HORNE'S IN ON IT TOO! WHO IS BLACK CAT, EH?

THE BLACK CAT JUST LOVES A GOOD CONTEST--OR A GOOD FIGHT! LET'S MEANDER DOWN TO THE POST OFFICE!

THE BLACK CAT ROARS THROUGH THE DARK STREETS AT BREAK NECK SPEED!

AFTER A PERIOD OF TENSE WAITING, TRUCKS PULL UP AND LOAD THE CONTEST MAIL AS RICK HORNE SUPERVISES--
HMM--RICK'S GOING ALONG WITH THOSE TRUCKS AND IF I FOLLOW, IT OUGHT TO LEAD ME TO WHOEVER'S BEHIND THIS CONTEST!

MILES LATER, ON A NARROW ROAD WINDING UP THE MOUNTAIN--

WHAT IN--? BLACK CAT?! HEY! IT'S ME--RICK!! WHAT'RE YOU DOING OUT HERE?
HOW INNOCENT HE CAN BE! NOW TO PUT ON SPEED AND CATCH--

ABRUPTLY!
OH-OH! THAT WAS CLOSE!
WHAT THE DEUCE! MY TIRE!
U.S.M.

AT FULL SPEED--OUT OF CONTROL!
I--I'M GOING TO-- YEEEEOWWWW!
RICK!!

RICKKKK! HE'LL BE KILLED!

(SOB)--OHHH--R-RICK DARLING! HE'S BARELY BREATHING--I'VE GOT TO RUSH HIM TO A DOCTOR, AND--

O-OH-H-- WHA-- BLACK CAT!
YES, RICK--ME! PFEW! YOU GAVE ME A SCARE! I THOUGHT YOU WERE--

HEY! WAIT UP! I--
NO TIME NOW, RICKIE BOY! I'M STILL PLAYING POST-OFFICE!

SPUTTERING EXHAUST OF A CAREENING MOTOR-CYCLE SHATTERS THE RURAL TRANQUILITY AS THE BLACK CAT RACES TO OVERTAKE THE TRUCKS--

THERE'RE THE TRUCKS--I'VE CAUGHT UP! AND THAT CHATEAU--IT'S LIKE THAT SET I HAD IN THE LADY OF THE LAKE--

A SCENE OF STORY-BOOK BEAUTY--

OH-OHH! THE BRIDGE--IT'S--
CREEEEEK!

I CAN'T MAKE IT!

OHHHHHHHHHH--

MEANWHILE, MILES AWAY-- FOOT-WEARY RICK PLODS DOGGEDLY TOWARD THE ROOK'S ROOST--

LATER-- I'M RICK HORNE! SO THIS IS THE ROOK'S PLACE! SAY, THAT'S A SHARP LITTLE OUTFIT! DIDN'T KNOW CLOTHES WERE THAT SCARCE!
THE MASTER EXPECTS YOU, SIR! FOLLOW, PLEASE!

INSIDE THE MAIN HALL AT THAT MOMENT---
HEY, ROOK! HOW YA SPELL "CAT"?
K-A-T, YA JOIK!
REALLY, GENTLEMEN, YOUR ERUDITION AMAZES ME! NOW FASTER WITH THE READING OF THE CONTEST ENTREES! SOMEWHERE IN THOSE STACKS MAY LIE THE ANSWER TO WHO IS THE BLACK CAT! FASTER!

DE WOIDS LOOKS BIGGER DIS WAY BUT DEY STILL AIN'T FAMILYER!

"--DE GOIL WHAT LIVES NEX' DOOR TO ME IS ALWAYS SWIPIN' DE MILK OFF ME DOORSTEP--MEBBE SHE'S DE BLACK CAT!"

MISTER RICK HORNE, MASTER!
AHH·· MR. HORNE! YOU'VE FINALLY ARRIVED! WELCOME TO MY HUMBLE ABODE··
HUMBLE? LOOKS MORE LIKE A DE MILLE SET! HOW'YA, ROOK! I SEE THE CONTEST MAIL GOT HERE OKAY··

WHO'RE THESE PUNKS, YOUR ASSISTANTS? WELL WHAT DO YOU KNOW! THERE'S SAMMY·· THE WEASEL··THE GATSEL·· WHY, THE WHOLE UNDERWORLD! WHAT GIVES, ROOK··THE MANPOWER SHORTAGE OR A CROOK CONVENTION?

YOU'RE A REASONABLY BRIGHT YOUNG MAN·· SUPPOSE YOU ANSWER THAT ONE YOURSELF!
DO I HAVE TO BOTHER?

SUIT YOURSELF! CHECKMATE HIM!

YEEOWWW

YOU AN' YER NUTTY IDEARS! DIS MAIL'S A LOAD OF JUNK!
YEAH! DERE AIN'T EVEN A GOOD CLUE TO WHO BLACK CAT IS IN ALL DESE LETTERS!
UNNERWOILD CHAMBER OF COMMERCE·· BUSHWA!!

SILENCE, LOWBROWS! REMEMBER, MY CHESSMEN KNOW THEIR PLACES!

THIS CONTEST--IF IT DOES NOTHING ELSE--WILL BRING HER TO ME!

WHILE OUTSIDE--AS THOUGH IN PROOF OF THE ROOK'S PROPHECY--
(GASP)--THAT FALL KNOCKED ME OUT FOR A WHILE, BUT--

I--I'M WARMING UP--STARTING TO FEEL BETTER ALREADY! NOW--FOR WHOEVER IT IS UP IN THERE WHO'S SO CURIOUS ABOUT MY REAL IDENTITY!

SECONDS LATER--
MASTER--L-LOOK!
WHA--AH-HA THE BLACK QUEEN! I KNEW IT! MY PLAN WORKED!

HA- HA- HA-- HAAAAA!
SAVE IT, MASTER MIND! I'D RATHER LAUGH LAST!

BAT HER BRAINS IN!
THERE'S T-TOO MANY OF T-THEM!
U-U-UUUHH..
I WANT HER ALIVE-- FOR A WHILE ANYWAY! STAND ASIDE! CHECK-MATE HER!!
LOOK OUT, BOYS--
THE TRAP IS SPRUNG!
THE FLOOR-- IT'S-- OOHHH..
R-RICKKK?
WELL, WHAT DO YOU KNOW? JUST LIKE OLD TIMES! DRAW UP A PIECE OF FLOOR AND SIT DOWN--
DO YOU ALWAYS HAVE TO CRACK WISE? MAYBE YOU DON'T REALIZE IT, BUT IF WE DON'T BREAK OUT WE'RE ANCIENT HISTORY! LEND A HAND-- IT'S OUR ONLY CHANCE!
THAT'S WHAT I LIKE ABOUT YOU, BLACK CAT, YOU'RE SO PRACTICAL!
MINUTES PASS--THEN DARINGLY INGENIOUS--
EXPOSE THE INNER CORE, RICK! ALL RIGHT--STAND BY!
BY YOU? FOR EVER AND EVER!

The FLASH OF A SHORT CIRCUIT BLAZES AGAINST THE OLD DOOR LOCK--

FREEDOM, AIN'T IT WONDERFUL?

YOU'VE STILL GOT TO HELP ME FIGHT FOR IT, SHARPIE! COME ON!

WON'T I?

WHO SAID-- YEEOWW! L-LOOK!

DA GUNS! SHE GOT DA GUNS!

CRIMINAL CELEBRATION, AS UNNOTICED--

DRINK, HEARTY TO MY SUCCESS, LADS! HA-HA! BLACK CAT WILL STIFLE OUR COMMERCE NO MORE!

SHE SURE WON'T ROOK! HAWW!

--AND THAT, LADIES AND GENTLEMEN, IS HOW BLACK CAT,--WITH THE AID OF YOUR HUMBLE SERVANT, NATCH',--BROKE UP THE VICIOUS UNDER-WORLD CHAMBER OF COMMERCE! AND NOW, LINDA TURNER, MY GUEST FOR TONIGHT! LINDA--WHO DO YOU THINK BLACK CAT REALLY IS?

I REALLY DON'T KNOW BUT WHO EVER SHE IS, DON'T YOU THINK SHE'S TERRIFIC?

KEEP THEM COVERED, RICK! I'LL PHONE THE POLICE!

HEY! COME BACK! I--I--WANT TO--

THE ADVENTURES OF PENROD

BY BOOTH TARKINGTON

CHAPTER XVIII
MUSIC

BOYHOOD IS THE LONGEST TIME IN LIFE for a boy. The last term of the school-year is made of decades, not of weeks, and living through them is like waiting for the millennium. But they do pass, somehow, and at last there came a day when Penrod was one of a group that capered out from the gravelled yard of "Ward School, Nomber Seventh," carolling a leave-taking of the institution, of their instructress, and not even forgetting Mr. Capps, the janitor.

> *"Good-bye, teacher! Good-bye, school! Good-bye, Cappsie, dern ole fool!"*

Penrod sang the loudest. For every boy, there is an age when he "finds his voice." Penrod's had not "changed," but he had found it. Inevitably that thing had come upon his family and the neighbours; and his father, a somewhat dyspeptic man, quoted frequently the expressive words of the "Lady of Shalott," but there were others whose sufferings were as poignant.

Vacation-time warmed the young of the world to pleasant languor; and a morning came that was like a brightly coloured picture in a child's fairy story. Miss Margaret Schofield, reclining in a hammock upon the front porch, was beautiful in the eyes of a newly made senior, well favoured and in fair raiment, beside her. A guitar rested lightly upon his knee, and he was trying to play—a matter of some difficulty, as the floor of the porch also seemed inclined to be musical. From directly under his feet came a voice of song, shrill, loud, incredibly piercing and incredibly flat, dwelling upon each syllable with incomprehensible reluctance to leave it.

> *"I have lands and earthly pow-wur.*
>
> *I'd give all for a now-wur,*
>
> *Whi-ilst setting at MY-Y-Y dear old mother's knee-ee,*
>
> *So-o-o rem-mem-bur whilst you're young—"*

Miss Schofield stamped heartily upon the musical floor.

"It's Penrod," she explained. "The lattice at the end of the porch is loose, and he crawls under and comes out all bugs. He's been having a dreadful singing fit lately—running away to picture shows and vaudeville, I suppose."

Mr. Robert Williams looked upon her yearningly. He touched a thrilling chord on his guitar and leaned nearer. "But you said you have missed me," he began. "I—"

The voice of Penrod drowned all other sounds.

"So-o-o rem-mem-bur, whi-i-ilst you're young,

That the day-a-ys to you will come,

When you're o-o-old and only in the way,

Do not scoff at them BEE-cause—"

"PENROD!" Miss Schofield stamped again.

"You DID say you'd missed me," said Mr. Robert Williams, seizing hurriedly upon the silence. "Didn't you say—"

A livelier tune rose upward.

"Oh, you talk about your fascinating beauties,

Of your dem-O-zells, your belles,

But the littil dame I met, while in the city,

She's par excellaws the queen of all the swells.

She's sweeter far—"

Margaret rose and jumped up and down repeatedly in a well-calculated area, whereupon the voice of Penrod cried chokedly, "QUIT that!" and there were subterranean coughings and sneezings.

"You want to choke a person to death?" he inquired severely, appearing at the end of the porch, a cobweb upon his brow. And, continuing, he put into practice a newly acquired phrase, "You better learn to be more considerick of other people's comfort."

Slowly and grievedly he withdrew, passed to the sunny side of the house, reclined in the warm grass beside his wistful Duke, and presently sang again.

"She's sweeter far than the flower I named her after,

And the memery of her smile it haunts me YET!

When in after years the moon is soffly beamun'

And at eve I smell the smell of mignonette

I will re-CALL that—"

"Pen-ROD!"

Mr. Schofield appeared at an open window upstairs, a book in his hand.

"Stop it!" he commanded. "Can't I stay home with a headache ONE morning from the office without having to listen to—I never DID hear such squawking!" He retired from the window, having too impulsively called upon his Maker. Penrod, shocked and injured, entered the house, but presently his voice was again audible as far as the front porch. He was holding converse with his mother, somewhere in the interior.

"Well, what of it? Sam Williams told me his mother said if Bob ever did think of getting married to Margaret, his mother said she'd like to know what in the name o' goodness they expect to—"

Bang! Margaret thought it better to close the front door.

The next minute Penrod opened it. "I suppose you want the whole family to get a sunstroke," he said reprovingly. "Keepin' every breath of air out o' the house on a day like this!"

And he sat down implacably in the doorway.

The serious poetry of all languages has omitted the little brother; and yet he is one of the great trials of love—the immemorial burden of courtship. Tragedy should have found place for him, but he has been left to the haphazard vignettist of Grub Street. He is the grave and real menace of lovers; his head is sacred and terrible, his power illimitable. There is one way—only one—to deal with him; but Robert Williams, having a brother of Penrod's age, understood that way.

Robert had one dollar in the world. He gave it to Penrod immediately.

Enslaved forever, the new Rockefeller rose and went forth upon the highway, an overflowing heart bursting the floodgates of song.

> *"In her eyes the light of love was softly gleamun',*
>
> *So sweetlay,*
>
> *So neatlay.*
>
> *On the banks the moon's soff light was brightly streamun',*
>
> *Words of love I then spoke TO her.*
>
> *She was purest of the PEW-er:*
>
> *'Littil sweetheart, do not sigh,*
>
> *Do not weep and do not cry.*
>
> *I will build a littil cottige just for yew-EW-EW and I.'"*

In fairness, it must be called to mind that boys older than Penrod have these wellings of pent melody; a wife can never tell when she is to undergo a musical morning, and even the golden wedding brings her no security, a man of ninety is liable to bust-loose in song, any time.

Invalids murmured pitifully as Penrod came within hearing; and people trying to think cursed the day that they were born, when he went shrilling by. His hands in his pockets, his shining face uplifted to the sky of June, he passed down the street, singing his way into the heart's deepest hatred of all who heard him.

> *"One evuning I was sturow-ling*
>
> *Midst the city of the DEAD,*

> *I viewed where all a-round me*
>
> *Their PEACE-full graves was SPREAD.*
>
> *But that which touched me mostlay—"*

He had reached his journey's end, a junk-dealer's shop wherein lay the long-desired treasure of his soul—an accordion which might have possessed a high quality of interest for an antiquarian, being unquestionably a ruin, beautiful in decay, and quite beyond the sacrilegious reach of the restorer. But it was still able to disgorge sounds—loud, strange, compelling sounds, which could be heard for a remarkable distance in all directions; and it had one rich calf-like tone that had gone to Penrod's heart. He obtained the instrument for twenty-two cents, a price long since agreed upon with the junk-dealer, who falsely claimed a loss of profit, Shylock that he was! He had found the wreck in an alley.

With this purchase suspended from his shoulder by a faded green cord, Penrod set out in a somewhat homeward direction, but not by the route he had just travelled, though his motive for the change was not humanitarian. It was his desire to display himself thus troubadouring to the gaze of Marjorie Jones. Heralding his advance by continuous experiments in the music of the future, he pranced upon his blithesome way, the faithful Duke at his heels. (It was easier for Duke than it would have been for a younger dog, because, with advancing age, he had begun to grow a little deaf.)

Turning the corner nearest to the glamoured mansion of the Joneses, the boy jongleur came suddenly face to face with Marjorie, and, in the delicious surprise of the encounter, ceased to play, his hands, in agitation, falling from the instrument.

Bareheaded, the sunshine glorious upon her amber curls, Marjorie was strolling hand-in-hand with her baby brother, Mitchell, four years old. She wore pink that day—unforgettable pink, with a broad, black patent-leather belt, shimmering reflections dancing upon its surface. How beautiful she was! How sacred the sweet little baby brother, whose privilege it was to cling to that small hand, delicately powdered with freckles.

"Hello, Marjorie," said Penrod, affecting carelessness.

"Hello!" said Marjorie, with unexpected cordiality. She bent over her baby brother with motherly affectations. "Say 'howdy' to the gentymuns, Mitchy-Mitch," she urged sweetly, turning him to face Penrod.

"WON'T!" said Mitchy-Mitch, and, to emphasize his refusal, kicked the gentymuns upon the shin.

Penrod's feelings underwent instant change, and in the sole occupation of disliking Mitchy-Mitch, he wasted precious seconds which might have been better employed in philosophic consideration of the startling example, just afforded, of how a given law operates throughout the universe in precisely the same manner perpetually. Mr. Robert Williams would have understood this, easily.

"Oh, oh!" Marjorie cried, and put Mitchy-Mitch behind her with too much sweetness. "Maurice Levy's gone to Atlantic City with his mamma," she remarked conversationally, as if the kicking incident were quite closed.

"That's nothin'," returned Penrod, keeping his eye uneasily upon Mitchy-Mitch. "I know plenty people been better places than that—Chicago and everywhere."

There was unconscious ingratitude in his low rating of Atlantic City, for it was largely to the attractions of that resort he owed Miss Jones' present attitude of friendliness.

Of course, too, she was curious about the accordion. It would be dastardly to hint that she had noticed a paper bag which bulged the pocket of Penrod's coat, and yet this bag was undeniably conspicuous—"and children are very like grown people sometimes!"

Penrod brought forth the bag, purchased on the way at a drug store, and till this moment UNOPENED, which expresses in a word the depth of his sentiment for Marjorie. It contained an abundant fifteen-cents' worth of lemon drops, jaw-breakers, licorice sticks, cinnamon drops, and shopworn choclate creams.

"Take all you want," he said, with off-hand generosity.

"Why, Penrod Schofield," exclaimed the wholly thawed damsel, "you nice boy!"

"Oh, that's nothin'," he returned airily. "I got a good deal of money, nowadays."

"Where from?"

"Oh—just around." With a cautious gesture he offered a jaw-breaker to Mitchy-Mitch, who snatched it indignantly and set about its absorption without delay.

"Can you play on that?" asked Marjorie, with some difficulty, her cheeks being rather too hilly for conversation.

"Want to hear me?"

She nodded, her eyes sweet with anticipation.

This was what he had come for. He threw back his head, lifted his eyes dreamily, as he had seen real musicians lift theirs, and distended the accordion preparing to produce the wonderful calf-like noise which was the instrument's great charm.

But the distention evoked a long wail which was at once drowned in another one.

"Ow! Owowaoh! Wowohah! Waow-WOW!" shrieked Mitchy-Mitch and the accordion together.

Mitchy-Mitch, to emphasize his disapproval of the accordion, opening his mouth still wider, lost therefrom the jaw-breaker, which rolled in the dust. Weeping, he stooped to retrieve it, and Marjorie, to prevent him, hastily set her foot upon it. Penrod offered another jaw-breaker; but Mitchy-Mitch struck it from his hand, desiring the former, which had convinced him of its sweetness.

Marjorie moved inadvertently; whereupon Mitchy-Mitch pounced upon the remains of his jaw-breaker and restored them, with accretions, to his mouth. His sister, uttering a cry of horror, sprang to the rescue, assisted by Penrod, whom she prevailed upon to hold Mitchy-Mitch's mouth open while she excavated. This operation being completed, and Penrod's right thumb severely bitten, Mitchy-Mitch closed his eyes tightly, stamped, squealed, bellowed, wrung his hands, and then, unexpectedly, kicked Penrod again.

Penrod put a hand in his pocket and drew forth a copper two-cent piece, large, round, and fairly bright.

He gave it to Mitchy-Mitch.

Mitchy-Mitch immediately stopped crying and gazed upon his benefactor with the eyes of a dog.

This world!

Thereafter did Penrod—with complete approval from Mitchy-Mitch—play the accordion for his lady to his heart's content, and hers. Never had he so won upon her; never had she let him feel so close to her before. They strolled up and down upon the sidewalk, eating, one thought between them, and soon she had learned to play the accordion almost as well as he. So passed a happy hour, which the Good King Rene of Anjou would have envied them, while Mitchy-Mitch made friends with Duke, romped about his sister and her swain, and clung to the hand of the latter, at intervals, with fondest affection and trust.

The noon whistles failed to disturb this little Arcady; only the sound of Mrs. Jones' voice for the third time summoning Marjorie and Mitchy-Mitch to lunch—sent Penrod on his way.

"I could come back this afternoon, I guess," he said, in parting.

"I'm not goin' to be here. I'm goin' to Baby Rennsdale's party."

Penrod looked blank, as she intended he should. Having thus satisfied herself, she added:

"There aren't goin' to be any boys there."

He was instantly radiant again.

"Marjorie—"

"Hum?"

"Do you wish I was goin' to be there?"

She looked shy, and turned away her head.

"MARJORIE JONES!" (This was a voice from home.) "HOW MANY MORE TIMES SHALL I HAVE TO CALL YOU?"

Marjorie moved away, her face still hidden from Penrod.

"Do you?" he urged.

At the gate, she turned quickly toward him, and said over her shoulder, all in a breath: "Yes! Come again to-morrow morning and I'll be on the corner. Bring your 'cordion!"

And she ran into the house, Mitchy-Mitch waving a loving hand to the boy on the sidewalk until the front door closed.

CHAPTER XIX
THE INNER BOY

PENROD WENT HOME IN SPLENDOUR, PRE-tending that he and Duke were a long procession; and he made enough noise to render the auricular part of the illusion perfect. His own family were already at the lunch-table when he arrived, and the parade halted only at the door of the dining-room.

"Oh SOMETHING!" shouted Mr. Schofield, clasping his bilious brow with both hands. "Stop that noise! Isn't it awful enough for you to SING? Sit DOWN! Not with that thing on! Take that green rope off your shoulder! Now take that thing out of the dining-room and throw it in the ash-can! Where did you get it?"

"Where did I get what, papa?" asked Penrod meekly, depositing the accordion in the hall just outside the dining-room door.

"That da—that third-hand concertina."

"It's a 'cordian," said Penrod, taking his place at the table, and noticing that both Margaret and Mr. Robert Williams (who happened to be a guest) were growing red.

"I don't care what you call it," said Mr. Schofield irritably. "I want to know where you got it."

Penrod's eyes met Margaret's: hers had a strained expression.

She very slightly shook her head. Penrod sent Mr. Williams a grateful look, and might have been startled if he could have seen himself in a mirror at that moment; for he regarded Mitchy-Mitch with concealed but vigorous aversion and the resemblance would have horrified him.

"A man gave it to me," he answered gently, and was rewarded by the visibly regained ease of his patron's manner, while Margaret leaned back in her chair and looked at her brother with real devotion.

"I should think he'd have been glad to," said Mr. Schofield. "Who was he?"

"Sir?" In spite of the candy which he had consumed in company with Marjorie and Mitchy-Mitch, Penrod had begun to eat lobster croquettes earnestly.

"Who WAS he?"

"Who do you mean, papa?"

"The man that gave you that ghastly Thing!"

"Yessir. A man gave it to me."

"I say, Who WAS he?" shouted Mr. Schofield.

"Well, I was just walking along, and the man came up to me—it was right down in front of Colgate's, where most of the paint's rubbed off the fence—"

"Penrod!" The father used his most dangerous tone.

"Sir?"

"Who was the man that gave you the concertina?"

"I don't know. I was walking along—"

"You never saw him before?"

"No, sir. I was just walk—"

"That will do," said Mr. Schofield, rising. "I suppose every family has its secret enemies and this was one of ours. I must ask to be excused!"

With that, he went out crossly, stopping in the hall a moment before passing beyond hearing. And, after lunch, Penrod sought in vain for his accordion; he even searched the library where his father sat reading, though, upon inquiry, Penrod explained that he was looking for a misplaced schoolbook. He thought he ought to study a little every day, he said, even during vacation-time. Much pleased, Mr. Schofield rose and joined the search, finding the missing work on mathematics with singular ease—which cost him precisely the price of the book the following September.

Penrod departed to study in the backyard. There, after a cautious survey of the neighbourhood, he managed to dislodge the iron cover of the cistern, and dropped the arithmetic within. A fine splash rewarded his listening ear. Thus assured that when he looked for that book again no one would find it for him, he replaced the cover, and betook himself pensively to the highway, discouraging Duke from following by repeated volleys of stones, some imaginary and others all too real.

Distant strains of brazen horns and the throbbing of drums were borne to him upon the kind breeze, reminding him that the world was made for joy, and that the Barzee and Potter Dog and Pony Show was exhibiting in a banlieue not far away. So, thither he bent his steps—the plentiful funds in his pocket burning hot holes all the way. He had paid twenty-two cents for the accordion, and fifteen for candy; he had bought the mercenary heart of Mitchy-Mitch for two: it certainly follows that there remained to him of his dollar, sixty-one cents—a fair fortune, and most unusual.

Arrived upon the populous and festive scene of the Dog and Pony Show, he first turned his attention to the brightly decorated booths which surrounded the tent. The cries of the peanut vendors, of the popcorn men, of the toy-balloon sellers, the stirring music of the band, playing before the performance to attract a crowd, the shouting of excited children and the barking of the dogs within the tent, all sounded exhilaratingly in Penrod's ears and set his blood a-tingle. Nevertheless, he did not squander his money or fling it to the winds in one grand splurge. Instead, he began cautiously with the purchase of an extraordinarily large pickle, which he obtained from an aged negress for his odd cent, too obvious a bargain to be missed. At an adjacent stand he bought a glass of raspberry lemonade (so alleged) and sipped it as he ate the pickle. He left nothing of either.

Next, he entered a small restaurant-tent and for a modest nickel was supplied with a fork and a box of sardines, previously opened, it is true, but more than half full. He consumed the sardines utterly, but left the tin box and the fork, after which he indulged in an inexpensive half-pint of lukewarm cider, at one of the open booths. Mug in hand, a gentle glow radiating toward his surface from various centres of activity deep inside him, he paused for breath—and the cool, sweet cadences of the watermelon man fell delectably upon his ear:

"Ice-cole WATER-melon; ice-cole water-MELON; the biggest slice of ICE-cole, ripe, red, ICE-cole, rich an' rare; the biggest slice of ice-cole watermelon ever cut by the hand of man! BUY our ICE-cole water-melon?"

Penrod, having drained the last drop of cider, complied with the watermelon man's luscious entreaty, and received a round slice of the fruit, magnificent in circumference and something over an inch in thickness. Leaving only the really dangerous part of the rind behind him, he wandered away from the vicinity of the watermelon man and supplied himself with a bag of peanuts, which, with the expenditure of a dime for admission, left a quarter still warm in his pocket. However, he managed to "break" the coin at a stand inside the tent, where a large, oblong paper box of popcorn was handed him, with twenty cents change. The box was too large to go into his pocket, but, having seated himself among some wistful Polack children, he placed it in his lap and devoured the contents at leisure during the performance. The popcorn was heavily larded with partially boiled molasses, and Penrod sandwiched mouthfuls of peanuts with gobs of this mass until the peanuts were all gone. After that, he ate with less avidity; a sense almost of satiety beginning to manifest itself to him, and it was not until the close of the performance that he disposed of the last morsel.

He descended a little heavily to the outflowing crowd in the arena, and bought a caterwauling toy balloon, but showed no great enthusiasm in manipulating it. Near the exit, as he came out, was a hot-waffle stand which he had overlooked, and a sense of duty obliged him to consume the three waffles, thickly powdered with sugar, which the waffle man cooked for him upon command.

They left a hottish taste in his mouth; they had not been quite up to his anticipation, indeed, and it was with a sense of relief that he turned to the "hokey-pokey" cart which stood close at hand, laden with square slabs of "Neapolitan ice-cream" wrapped in paper. He thought the ice-cream would be cooling, but somehow it fell short of the desired effect, and left a peculiar savour in his throat.

He walked away, too languid to blow his balloon, and passed a fresh-taffy booth with strange indifference. A bare-armed man was manipulating the taffy over a hook, pulling a great white mass to the desired stage of "candying," but Penrod did not pause to watch the operation; in fact, he averted his eyes (which were slightly glazed) in passing. He did not analyze his motives: simply, he was conscious that he preferred not to look at the mass of taffy.

For some reason, he put a considerable distance between himself and the taffy-stand, but before long halted in the presence of a red-faced man who flourished a long fork over a small cooking apparatus and shouted jovially: "Winnies! HERE'S your hot winnies! Hot winny-WURST! Food for the over-worked brain, nourishing for the weak stummick, entertaining for the tired business man! HERE'S your hot winnies, three for a nickel, a half-a-dime, the twentieth-pot-of-a-dollah!"

This, above all nectar and ambrosia, was the favourite dish of Penrod Schofield. Nothing inside him now craved it—on the contrary! But memory is the great hypnotist; his mind argued against his inwards that opportunity knocked at his door: "winny-wurst" was rigidly forbidden by the home authorities. Besides, there was a last nickel in his pocket; and nature protested against its survival. Also, the redfaced man had himself proclaimed his wares nourishing for the weak stummick.

Penrod placed the nickel in the red hand of the red-faced man.

He ate two of the three greasy, cigarlike shapes cordially pressed upon him in return. The first bite convinced him that he had made a mistake; these winnies seemed of a very inferior flavour, almost unpleasant, in fact. But he felt obliged to conceal his poor opinion of them, for fear of offending the red-faced man. He ate without haste or eagerness—so slowly, indeed, that he began to think the red-faced man might dislike him, as a deterrent of trade. Perhaps Penrod's mind was not working well, for he failed to remember that no law compelled him to remain under the eye of the red-faced man, but the virulent repulsion excited by his attempt to take a bite of the third sausage inspired him with at least an excuse for postponement.

"Mighty good," he murmured feebly, placing the sausage in the pocket of his jacket with a shaking hand. "Guess I'll save this one to eat at home, after—after dinner."

He moved sluggishly away, wishing he had not thought of dinner. A side-show, undiscovered until now, failed to arouse his interest, not even exciting a wish that he had known of its existence when he had money. For a time he stared without attraction; the weather-worn colours conveying no meaning to comprehension at a

HERE YOU ARE · ALL HOT

huge canvas poster depicting the chief his torpid eye. Then, little by little, the poster became more vivid to his consciousness. There was a greenish-tinted person in the tent, it seemed, who thrived upon a reptilian diet.

Suddenly, Penrod decided that it was time to go home.

CHAPTER XX
BROTHERS OF
ANGELS

"Indeed, doctor," said Mrs. Schofield, with agitation and profound conviction, just after eight o'clock that evening, "I shall ALWAYS believe in mustard plasters—mustard plasters and hot—water bags. If it hadn't been for them I don't believed he'd have LIVED till you got here—I do NOT!"

"Margaret," called Mr. Schofield from the open door of a bedroom, "Margaret, where did you put that aromatic ammonia? Where's Margaret?"

But he had to find the aromatic spirits of ammonia himself, for Margaret was not in the house. She stood in the shadow beneath a maple tree near the street corner, a guitar-case in her hand; and she scanned with anxiety a briskly approaching figure. The arc light, swinging above, revealed this figure as that of him she awaited. He was passing toward the gate without seeing her, when she arrested him with a fateful whisper.

"BOB!"

Mr. Robert Williams swung about hastily. "Why, Margaret!"

"Here, take your guitar," she whispered hurriedly. "I was afraid if father happened to find it he'd break it all to pieces!"

"What for?" asked the startled Robert.

"Because I'm sure he knows it's yours." "But what—"

"Oh, Bob," she moaned, "I was waiting here to tell you. I was so afraid you'd try to come in—"

"TRY!" exclaimed the unfortunate young man, quite dumfounded. "TRY to come—"

"Yes, before I warned you. I've been waiting here to tell you, Bob, you mustn't come near the house if I were you I'd stay away from even this neighbourhood—far away! For a while I don't think it would be actually SAFE for—"

"Margaret, will you please—"

"It's all on account of that dollar you gave Penrod this morning," she walled. "First, he bought that horrible concertina that made papa so furious—"

"But Penrod didn't tell that I—"

"Oh, wait!" she cried lamentably. "Listen! He didn't tell at lunch, but he got home about dinner-time in the most—well! I've seen pale people before, but nothing like Penrod. Nobody could IMAGINE it—not unless they'd seen him! And he looked, so STRANGE, and kept making such unnatural faces, and at first all he would say was that he'd eaten a little piece of apple and thought it must have some microbes on it. But he got sicker and sicker, and we put him to bed—and then we all thought he was going to die—and, of COURSE, no little piece of apple would have—well, and he kept getting worse and then he said he'd had a dollar. He said he'd spent it for the concertina, and watermelon, and chocolate-creams, and licorice sticks, and lemon-drops, and peanuts, and jaw-breakers, and sardines, and raspberry lemonade, and pickles, and popcorn, and ice-cream, and cider, and sausage—there was sausage in his pocket, and mamma says his jacket is ruined—and cinnamon drops—and waffles—and he ate four or five lobster croquettes at lunch—and papa said, 'Who gave you that dollar?' Only he didn't say 'WHO'—he said something horrible, Bob! And Penrod thought he was going to die, and he said you gave it to him, and oh! it was just pitiful to hear the poor child, Bob, because he thought he was dying, you see, and he blamed you for the whole thing. He said if you'd only let him alone and not given it to him, he'd have grown up to be a good man—and now he couldn't! I never heard anything so heart-rending—he was so weak he could hardly whisper, but he kept trying to talk, telling us over and over it was all your fault."

In the darkness Mr. Williams' facial expression could not be seen, but his voice sounded hopeful.

"Is he—is he still in a great deal of pain?"

"They say the crisis is past," said Margaret, "but the doctor's still up there. He said it was the acutest case of indigestion he had ever treated in the whole course of his professional practice."

"Of course *I* didn't know what he'd do with the dollar," said Robert.

She did not reply.

He began plaintively, "Margaret, you don't—"

"I've never seen papa and mamma so upset about anything," she said, rather primly.

"You mean they're upset about ME?"

"We ARE all very much upset," returned Margaret, more starch in her tone as she remembered not only Penrod's sufferings but a duty she had vowed herself to perform.

"Margaret! YOU don't—"

"Robert," she said firmly and, also, with a rhetorical complexity which breeds a suspicion of pre-rehearsal—"Robert, for the present I can only look at it in one way: when you gave that money to Penrod you put into the hands of an unthinking little child a weapon which might be,

and, indeed, was, the means of his undoing. Boys are not respon—"

"But you saw me give him the dollar, and you didn't—"

"Robert!" she checked him with increasing severity. "I am only a woman and not accustomed to thinking everything out on the spur of the moment; but I cannot change my mind. Not now, at least."

"And you think I'd better not come in to-night?"

"To-night!" she gasped. "Not for WEEKS! Papa would—"

"But Margaret," he urged plaintively, "how can you blame me for—"

"I have not used the word 'blame,'" she interrupted. "But I must insist that for your carelessness to—to wreak such havoc—cannot fail to—to lessen my confidence in your powers of judgment. I cannot change my convictions in this matter—not to-night—and I cannot remain here another instant. The poor child may need me. Robert, good-night."

With chill dignity she withdrew, entered the house, and returned to the sick-room, leaving the young man in outer darkness to brood upon his crime—and upon Penrod.

That sincere invalid became convalescent upon the third day; and a week elapsed, then, before he found an opportunity to leave the house unaccompanied—save by Duke. But at last he set forth and approached the Jones neighbourhood in high spirits, pleasantly conscious of his pallor, hollow cheeks, and other perquisites of illness provocative of interest.

One thought troubled him a little because it gave him a sense of inferiority to a rival. He believed, against his will, that Maurice Levy could have successfully eaten chocolate-creams, licorice sticks, lemon-drops, jaw-breakers, peanuts, waffles, lobster croquettes, sardines, cinnamon-drops, watermelon, pickles, popcorn, ice-cream and sausage with raspberry lemonade and cider. Penrod had admitted to himself that Maurice could do it and afterward attend to business, or pleasure, without the slightest discomfort; and this was probably no more than a fair estimate of one of the great constitutions of all time. As a digester, Maurice Levy would have disappointed a Borgia.

Fortunately, Maurice was still at Atlantic City—and now the convalescent's heart leaped. In the distance he saw Marjorie coming—in pink again, with a ravishing little parasol over her head. And alone! No Mitchy-Mitch was to mar this meeting.

Penrod increased the feebleness of his steps, now and then leaning upon the fence as if for support.

"How do you do, Marjorie?" he said, in his best sick-room voice, as she came near.

To his pained amazement, she proceeded on her way, her nose at a celebrated elevation—an icy nose.

She cut him dead.

He threw his invalid's airs to the winds, and hastened after her.

"Marjorie," he pleaded, "what's the matter? Are you mad? Honest, that day you said to come back next morning, and you'd be on the corner, I was sick. Honest, I was AWFUL sick, Marjorie! I had to have the doctor—"

"DOCTOR!" She whirled upon him, her lovely eyes blazing.

"I guess WE'VE had to have the doctor enough at OUR house, thanks to you, Mister Penrod Schofield. Papa says you haven't got NEAR sense enough to come in out of the rain, after what you did to poor little Mitchy-Mitch—"

"What?"

"Yes, and he's sick in bed YET!" Marjorie went on, with unabated fury. "And papa says if he ever catches you in this part of town—"

"WHAT'D I do to Mitchy-Mitch?" gasped Penrod.

"You know well enough what you did to Mitchy-Mitch!" she cried. "You gave him that great, big, nasty two-cent piece!"

"Well, what of it?"

"Mitchy-Mitch swallowed it!"

"What!"

"And papa says if he ever just lays eyes on you, once, in this neighbourhood—"

But Penrod had started for home.

In his embittered heart there was increasing a critical disapproval of the Creator's methods. When He made pretty girls, thought Penrod, why couldn't He have left out their little brothers!

TO BE CONTINUED IN LITERARY OUTLAW #7

Chapter 2. AHAB APPEARS

TWO HOURS BEFORE THE FLOOD TIDE ... IT WOULD THEN BE AROUND THE THIRD BELL OF THE AFTERNOON WATCH ... ISHMAEL AND QUEEQUEG WENT ABOARD THEIR NEW SHIP AND STOWED THEIR GEAR IN THE FORECASTLE. IT WAS EMPTY, SAVE FOR A SINGLE OLD SAILOR ASLEEP ON HIS STOMACH ACROSS TWO SEA CHESTS ...

ISHMAEL WAS ABOUT TO QUESTION CLEGGER ABOUT THE STRANGE CAPTAIN AHAB ... BUT, SUDDENLY THERE WAS A NOISE ON DECK, AND A BEWHISKERED BO'SUN STUCK HIS HEAD IN THE DOORWAY ...

Moby Dick

14
ON DECK WAS A SCENE OF ORDERLY CONFUSION AS A HEAVY THREE-INCH HAWSER WAS BEING MANHANDLED TO THE MAIN CAPSTAN. ISHMAEL AND HIS COMRADE TOOK THEIR PLACES ON THE HAWSER... AND THE SEAFARING SCHOOLMASTER FOUND TIME TO CAST A GLANCE TOWARDS THE QUARTERDECK...
I DON'T SEE CAPTAIN AHAB AROUND.
NOR WILL YOU, NOT YET AWHILE, HE'S KEEPING CLOSE TO HIS CABIN. THEY SAY HE'S SICK, THOUGH HE DON'T LOOK SO, JUST MOODY—DESPERATE MOODY—SAVAGE MOODY!

PRESENTLY, HAVING BEEN HAULED CLEAR OF THE PRESS OF ANCHORED SHIPPING BY A PAIR OF HARBOUR CUTTERS, THE "PEQUOD" CAST OFF HER TOW ROPES...
TOPMEN ALOFT! SET TOPS'LS AND JIBS!
TOWS GONE!

Moby Dick

15

OUT PAST THE MOLE, ROUND THE WAILING BUOY, WITH THE MUDDY BROWN WATER CREAMING BENEATH HER IRON-BOUND STEM..."PEQUOD" HEELED TO MEET A SNAPPY SOU'WESTER.
FIVE POINTS ON THE PORT BOW LAY THE END OF NANTUCKET SOUND... AHEAD LAY THE BROAD ATLANTIC... AND THE BREATHTAKING ADVENTURE OF THE WHALE HUNT!

MEET HER! STEADY AS YOU GO!

BEING BORNE ON THE SHIP'S BOOKS AS A SEAMAN AND SAIL-WORKER, ISHMAEL MADE EARLY ACQUAINTANCE OF STARBUCK, THE CHIEF MATE OF THE "PEQUOD", A KEEN-EYED, TACITURN WHALING MAN OF THE OLD BREED...

YOU'LL BE MAINTOP — GET ALOFT AND REPORT TO WIGERY... HE'LL GIVE YOU YER ORDERS.

AYE, AYE.

Moby Dick

16

IT WAS OVER A YEAR SINCE ISHMAEL HAD SWARMED UP TARRY MAINMAST SHROUDS WITH A SHIP HEELING TREACHEROUSLY BENEATH HIM ... AS HE CLIMBED, HE FELT A FLOOD OF ELATION SURGING THROUGH HIS VEINS — NOT UNMIXED WITH UNEASE.

AT SEA IN A WHALING SHIP.... WHAT MANNER OF ADVENTURE LIES AHEAD OF ME? AND THIS PEQUOD, WHAT OF HER? AND WHAT OF THE MYSTERIOUS CAPTAIN AHAB WHO KEEPS CLOSE TO HIS CABIN, SAVAGE MOODY?

WIGERY, THE CAPTAIN OF THE MAINTOP, WAS BELLOWING ORDERS AGAINST A BREATH-ROBBING GALE OF WIND ... HE PAUSED AS ISHMAEL MADE HIMSELF KNOWN.

NEW MAINTOPMAN, EH? HEAVEN HELP YOU IF YOU'RE NO BETTER HAND THAN YONDER CHUCKLE-HEADED, MUTTON-FISTED SWABS — *ALOFT TO THE TOPGALLANT WITH YOU — HELP REEF!*

AYE, AYE!

Moby Dick
17

REEFING DOWN A MAIN TOPGALLANT SAIL IN A FORTY MILE AN HOUR NANTUCKET SOU'WESTER, WITH THE MASTHEAD SWINGING THROUGH FIFTY DEGREES AND NOTHING BUT A FOOTHOLD ON A SLENDER RATLINE, WAS NO MEAN TASK...
NAME O' GEACH! — HOWDY!
NAME OF ISHMAEL! — HOWDY!

BLEEDING HANDS AND TORN FINGERNAILS TRIUMPHED OVER THE WILDLY-FLAPPING, SALT-HARDENED CANVAS... AND ISHMAEL'S COMPANION FLASHED A TOOTHLESS GRIN...
SEEN AUGHT O' CAP'N AHAB YET?
NOT YET—
YOU'LL SEE HIM SOON ENOUGH — AN' THAT'LL BE TOO SOON!

Moby Dick
18
RETURNING TO THE DECK WITH THE TASK COMPLETED, ISHMAEL SOUGHT OUT HIS COMRADE, QUEEQUEG. HE FOUND THE DARK-SKINNED HARPOONER LISTENING OPEN-MOUTHED TO THE FIRST MATE WHO WAS BERATING VARIOUS MEMBERS OF THE CREW...
YOU MAY SPEAK OF YOUR SKILL AND YOUR COURAGE, BUT LET ME TELL YOU THIS! WHEN WE GET TO THE SOUTHERN SEA AND THE WHALES ARE A-BLOW, I'LL BE CHOOSING MY WHALEBOAT'S CREW CAREFULLY...
HIS LONG, BONY FINGER STABBED AT QUEEQUEG...
YOU! HEATHEN! TELL ME SWIFTLY— ARE YOU AFRAID OF A WHALE?
QUEEQUEG NO LIKING TELLEE LIE—DEM WHALE SCARE QUEEQUEG PLENTY GOOD, YOU BET!
Moby Dick

Moby Dick
19
STARBUCK'S EYES FLASHED TRIUMPH...
A MAN AFTER MY OWN HEART! YOU'RE THE HARPOONER FOR ME ON THIS VOYAGE, HEATHEN.... NO DANGEROUS, FOOLHARDY SWAB FOR ME... TWENTY YEARS O' WHALING HAVE TAUGHT ME ONE THING -- I'LL HAVE NO MAN IN MY BOAT WHO'S NOT AFRAID OF A WHALE!

THE FIRST MATE WAS ABOUT TO ADD TO THIS SHAFT OF WISDOM WHEN HIS EYES BY-PASSED QUEEQUEG. SUDDENLY, HIS WHOLE ATTITUDE CHANGED...
LOOK TO YOUR TASKS ALL OF YOU. THE CAP'N'S JUST COME ON DECK!

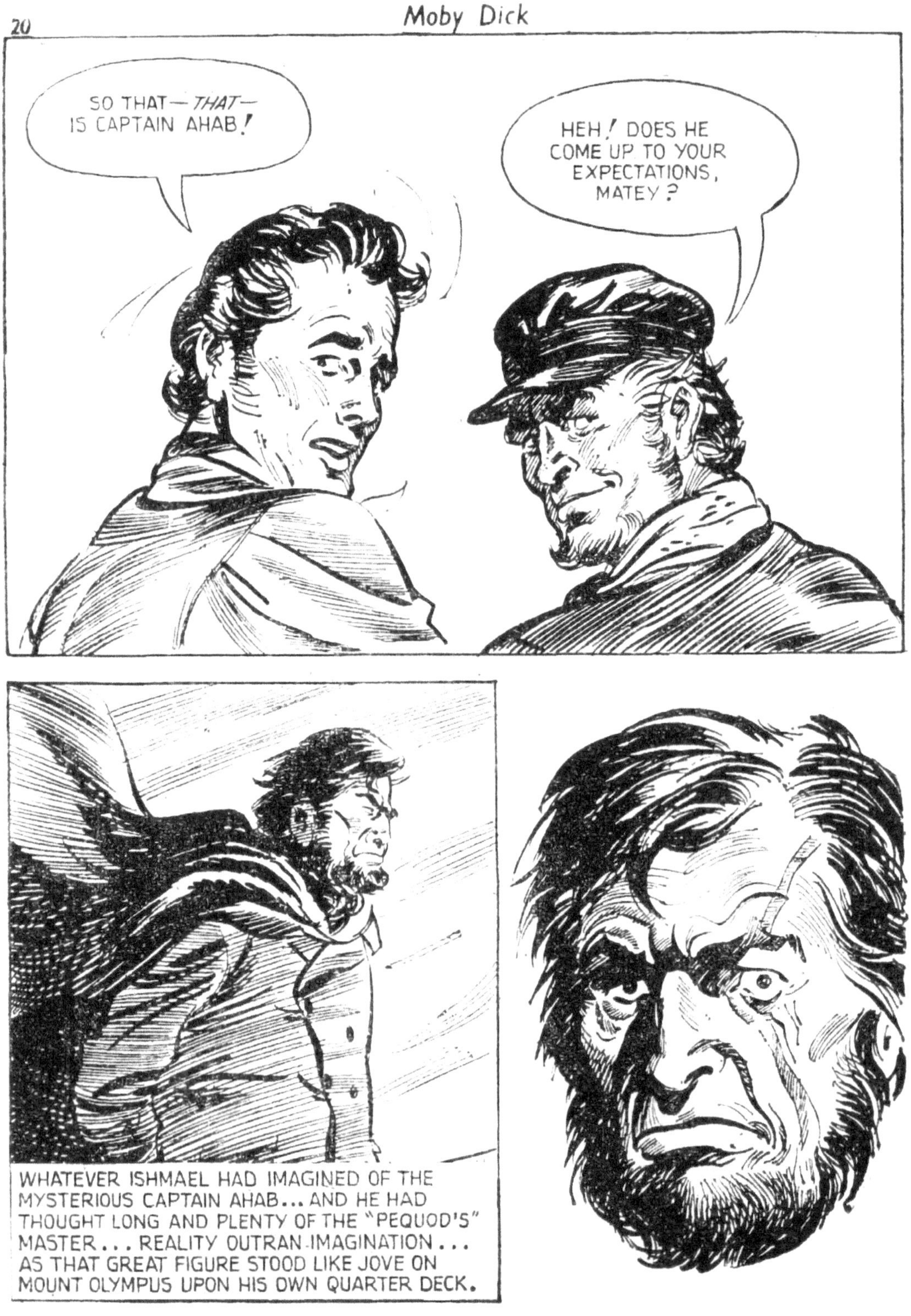

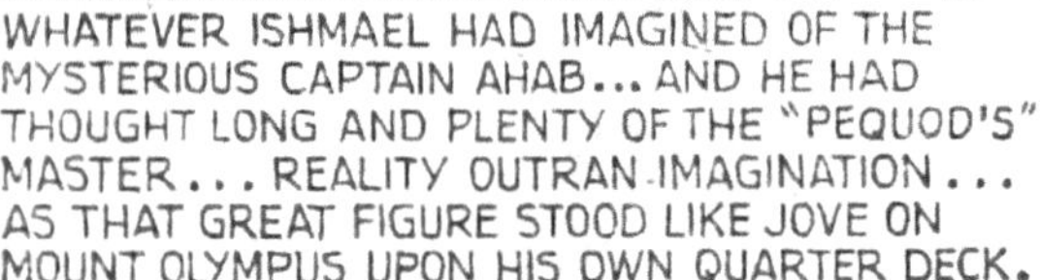

WHATEVER ISHMAEL HAD IMAGINED OF THE MYSTERIOUS CAPTAIN AHAB... AND HE HAD THOUGHT LONG AND PLENTY OF THE "PEQUOD'S" MASTER... REALITY OUTRAN IMAGINATION... AS THAT GREAT FIGURE STOOD LIKE JOVE ON MOUNT OLYMPUS UPON HIS OWN QUARTER DECK.

NYARLATHOTEP

BY H. P. LOVECRAFT

NYARLATHOTEP . . . THE CRAWLING CHAOS . . . I am the last . . . I will tell the audient void. . . .

I do not recall distinctly when it began, but it was months ago. The general tension was horrible. To a season of political and social upheaval was added a strange and brooding apprehension of hideous physical danger; a danger widespread and all-embracing, such a danger as may be imagined only in the most terrible phantasms of the night. I recall that the people went about with pale and worried faces, and whispered warnings and prophecies which no one dared consciously repeat or acknowledge to himself that he had heard. A sense of monstrous guilt was upon the land, and out of the abysses between the stars swept chill currents that made men shiver in dark and lonely places. There was a daemoniac alteration in the sequence of the seasons—the autumn heat lingered fearsomely, and everyone felt that the world and perhaps the universe had passed from the control of known gods or forces to that of gods or forces which were unknown.

And it was then that Nyarlathotep came out of Egypt. Who he was, none could tell, but he was of the old native blood and looked like a Pharaoh. The fellahin knelt when they saw him, yet could not say why. He said he had risen up out of the blackness of twenty-seven centuries, and that he had heard messages from places not on this planet. Into the lands of civilisation came Nyarlathotep, swarthy, slender, and sinister, always buying strange instruments of glass and metal and combining them into instruments yet stranger. He spoke much of the sciences—of electricity and psychology—and gave exhibitions of power which sent his spectators away speechless, yet which swelled his fame to exceeding magnitude. Men advised one another to see Nyarlathotep, and shuddered. And where Nyarlathotep went, rest vanished; for the small hours were rent with the screams of nightmare. Never before had the screams of nightmare been such a public problem; now the wise men almost wished they could forbid sleep in the small hours, that the shrieks of cities might less horribly disturb the pale, pitying moon as it glimmered on green waters gliding under bridges, and old steeples crumbling against a sickly sky.

I remember when Nyarlathotep came to my city—the great, the old, the terrible city of unnumbered crimes. My friend had told me of him, and of the impelling fascination and allurement of his revelations, and I burned with eagerness to explore his uttermost mysteries. My friend said they were horrible and impressive beyond my most fevered imaginings; that what was thrown on a screen in the darkened room prophesied things none but Nyarlathotep dared prophesy, and that in the sputter of his sparks there was taken from men that which had never been taken before yet which shewed only in the eyes. And I heard it hinted abroad that those who knew Nyarlathotep looked on sights which others saw not.

It was in the hot autumn that I went through the night with the restless crowds to see Nyarlathotep; through the stifling night and up the endless stairs into the choking room. And shadowed on a screen, I saw hooded forms amidst ruins, and yellow evil faces peering from behind fallen monuments. And I saw the world battling against blackness; against the waves of destruction from ultimate space; whirling, churning; struggling around the dimming, cooling sun. Then the sparks played amazingly around the heads of the spectators, and hair stood up on end whilst shadows more grotesque than I can tell came out and squatted on the heads. And when I, who was colder and more scientific than the rest, mumbled a trembling protest about "imposture" and "static electricity", Nyarlathotep drave us all out, down the dizzy stairs into the damp, hot, deserted midnight streets. I screamed aloud that I was not afraid; that I never could be afraid; and others screamed with me for solace. We sware to one another that the city was exactly the same, and still alive; and when the electric lights began to fade we cursed the company over and over again, and laughed at the queer faces we made.

I believe we felt something coming down from the greenish moon, for when we began to depend on its light we drifted into curious involuntary formations and seemed to know our destinations though we dared not think of them. Once we looked at the pavement and found the blocks loose and displaced by grass, with scarce a line of rusted metal to shew where the tramways had run. And again we saw a tram-car, lone, windowless, dilapidated, and almost on its side. When we gazed around the horizon, we could not find the third tower by the river, and noticed that the silhouette of the second tower was ragged at the top. Then we split up into narrow columns, each of which seemed drawn in a different direction. One disappeared in a narrow alley to the left, leaving only the echo of a shocking moan. Another filed down a weed-choked subway entrance, howling with a laughter that was mad. My own column was sucked toward the open country, and presently felt a chill which was not of the hot autumn; for as we stalked out on the dark moor, we beheld around us the hellish moon-glitter of evil snows. Trackless, inexplicable snows, swept asunder in one direction only, where lay a gulf all the blacker for its glittering walls. The column seemed very thin indeed as it plodded dreamily into the gulf. I lingered behind, for the black rift in the green-litten snow was frightful, and I thought I had heard the reverberations of a disquieting wail as my companions vanished; but my power to linger was slight. As if beckoned by those who had gone before, I half floated between the titanic snowdrifts, quivering and afraid, into the sightless vortex of the unimaginable.

Screamingly sentient, dumbly delirious, only the gods that were can tell. A sickened, sensitive shadow writhing in hands that are not hands, and whirled blindly past ghastly midnights of rotting creation, corpses of dead worlds with sores that were cities, charnel winds that brush the pallid stars and make them flicker low. Beyond the worlds vague ghosts of monstrous things; half-seen columns of unsanctified temples that rest on nameless rocks beneath space and reach up to dizzy vacua above the spheres of light and darkness. And through this revolting graveyard of the universe the muffled, maddening beating of drums, and thin, monotonous whine of blasphemous flutes from inconceivable, unlighted chambers beyond Time; the detestable pounding and piping whereunto dance slowly, awkwardly, and absurdly the gigantic, tenebrous ultimate gods—the blind, voiceless, mindless gargoyles whose soul is Nyarlathotep.

THE END

THE DREAMS IN THE WITCH HOUSE

BY H. P. LOVECRAFT

WHETHER THE DREAMS BROUGHT ON THE fever or the fever brought on the dreams Walter Gilman did not know. Behind everything crouched the brooding, festering horror of the ancient town, and of the mouldy, unhallowed garret gable where he wrote and studied and wrestled with figures and formulae when he was not tossing on the meagre iron bed. His ears were growing sensitive to a preternatural and intolerable degree, and he had long ago stopped the cheap mantel clock whose ticking had come to seem like a thunder of artillery. At night the subtle stirring of the black city outside, the sinister scurrying of rats in the wormy partitions, and the creaking of hidden timbers in the centuried house, were enough to give him a sense of strident pandemonium. The darkness always teemed with unexplained sound—and yet he sometimes shook with fear lest the noises he heard should subside and allow him to hear certain other, fainter, noises which he suspected were lurking behind them.

He was in the changeless, legend-haunted city of Arkham, with its clustering gambrel roofs that sway and sag over attics where witches hid from the King's men in the dark, olden days of the Province. Nor was any spot in that city more steeped in macabre memory than the gable room which harboured him—for it was this house and this room which had likewise harboured old Keziah Mason, whose flight from Salem Gaol at the last no one was ever able to explain. That was in 1692—the gaoler had gone mad and babbled of a small, white-fanged furry thing which scuttled out of Keziah's cell, and not even Cotton Mather could explain the curves and angles smeared on the grey stone walls with some red, sticky fluid.

Possibly Gilman ought not to have studied so hard. Non-Euclidean calculus and quantum physics are enough to stretch any brain; and when one mixes them with folklore, and tries to trace a strange background of multi-dimensional reality behind the ghoulish hints of the Gothic tales and the wild whispers of the chimney-corner, one can hardly expect to be wholly free from mental tension. Gilman came from Haverhill, but it was only after he had entered college in Arkham that he began to connect his mathematics with the fantastic legends of elder magic. Something in the air of the hoary town worked obscurely on his imagination. The professors at Miskatonic had urged him to slacken up, and had voluntarily cut down his course at several points. Moreover, they had stopped him from consulting the dubious old books on forbidden secrets that were kept under lock and key in a vault at the university library. But all these precautions came late in the

day, so that Gilman had some terrible hints from the dreaded Necronomicon of Abdul Alhazred, the fragmentary Book of Eibon, and the suppressed Unaussprechlichen Kulten of von Junzt to correlate with his abstract formulae on the properties of space and the linkage of dimensions known and unknown.

He knew his room was in the old Witch House—that, indeed, was why he had taken it. There was much in the Essex County records about Keziah Mason's trial, and what she had admitted under pressure to the Court of Oyer and Terminer had fascinated Gilman beyond all reason. She had told Judge Hathorne of lines and curves that could be made to point out directions leading through the walls of space to other spaces beyond, and had implied that such lines and curves were frequently used at certain midnight meetings in the dark valley of the white stone beyond Meadow Hill and on the unpeopled island in the river. She had spoken also of the Black Man, of her oath, and of her new secret name of Nahab. Then she had drawn those devices on the walls of her cell and vanished.

Gilman believed strange things about Keziah, and had felt a queer thrill on learning that her dwelling was still standing after more than 235 years. When he heard the hushed Arkham whispers about Keziah's persistent presence in the old house and the narrow streets, about the irregular human tooth-marks left on certain sleepers in that and other houses, about the childish cries heard near May-Eve, and Hallowmass, about the stench often noted in the old house's attic just after those dreaded seasons, and about the small, furry, sharp-toothed thing which haunted the mouldering structure and the town and nuzzled people curiously in the black hours before dawn, he resolved to live in the place at any cost. A room was easy to secure; for the house was unpopular, hard to rent, and long given over to cheap lodgings. Gilman could not have told what he expected to find there, but he knew he wanted to be in the building where some circumstance had more or less suddenly given a mediocre old woman of the seventeenth century an insight into mathematical depths perhaps beyond the utmost modern delvings of Planck, Heisenberg, Einstein, and de Sitter.

He studied the timber and plaster walls for traces of cryptic designs at every accessible spot where the paper had peeled, and within a week managed to get the eastern attic room where Keziah was held to have practiced her spells. It had been vacant from the first—for no one had ever been willing to stay there long—but the Polish landlord had grown wary about renting it. Yet nothing whatever happened to Gilman till about the time of the fever. No ghostly Keziah flitted through the sombre halls and chambers, no small furry thing crept into his dismal eyrie to nuzzle him, and no record of the witch's incantations rewarded his constant search. Sometimes he would take walks through shadowy tangles of unpaved musty-smelling lanes where eldritch brown houses of unknown age leaned and tottered and leered mockingly through narrow, small-paned windows. Here he knew strange things had happened once, and there was a faint suggestion behind the surface that everything of that monstrous past might not—at least in the darkest, narrowest, and most intricately crooked alleys—have utterly perished. He also rowed out twice to the ill-regarded island in the river, and made a sketch of the singular angles described by the moss-grown rows of grey standing stones whose origin was so obscure and immemorial.

Gilman's room was of good size but queerly irregular shape; the north wall slanting perceptibly inward from the outer to the inner end, while the low ceiling slanted gently downward in the same direction. Aside from an obvious rat-hole and the signs of other stopped-up ones, there was no access—nor any appearance of a former avenue of access—to the space which must have existed between the slanting wall and the straight outer wall on the house's north side, though a view from the exterior shewed where a window had been boarded up at a very remote date. The loft above the ceiling—which must have had a slanting floor—was likewise inaccessible. When Gilman climbed up a ladder to the cobwebbed level loft above the rest of the attic he found vestiges of a bygone aperture tightly and heavily covered with ancient planking and secured by the stout wooden pegs common in colonial carpentry. No amount of persuasion, however, could induce the stolid landlord to let him investigate either of these two closed spaces.

As time wore along, his absorption in the irregular wall and ceiling of his room increased; for he began to read into the odd angles a mathematical significance which seemed to offer vague clues regarding their purpose. Old Keziah, he reflected, might have had excellent reasons for living in a room with peculiar angles; for was it not through certain angles that she claimed to have gone outside the boundaries of the world of space we know? His interest gradually veered away from the unplumbed voids beyond the slanting surfaces, since it now appeared that the purpose of those surfaces concerned the side he was already on.

The touch of brain-fever and the dreams began early in February. For some time, apparently, the curious angles of Gilman's room had been having a strange, almost hypnotic effect on him; and as the bleak winter advanced he had found himself staring more and more intently at the corner where the down-slanting ceiling met the inward-slanting wall. About this period his inability to concentrate on his formal studies worried him considerably, his apprehensions about the mid-year examinations being very acute. But the exaggerated sense of hearing was scarcely less annoying. Life had become an insistent and almost unendurable cacophony, and there was that constant, terrifying impression of other sounds—perhaps from regions beyond life—trembling on the very brink of audibility. So far as concrete noises went, the rats in the ancient partitions were the worst. Sometimes their scratching seemed not only furtive but deliberate. When it came from beyond the slanting north wall it was mixed with a sort of dry rattling—and when it came from the century-closed loft above the slanting ceiling Gilman always braced himself as if expecting some horror which only bided its time before descending to engulf him utterly.

The dreams were wholly beyond the pale of sanity, and Gilman felt that they must be a result, jointly, of his studies in mathematics and in folklore. He had been thinking too much about the vague regions which his formulae told him must lie beyond the three dimensions we know, and about the possibility that old Keziah Mason—guided by some influence past all conjecture—had actually found the gate to those regions. The yellowed county records containing her testimony and that of her accusers were so damnably suggestive of things beyond human experience—and the descriptions of the darting little furry object which served as her familiar were so painfully realistic despite their incredible details.

That object—no larger than a good-sized rat and quaintly called by the townspeople "Brown Jenkin"—seemed to have been the fruit of a remarkable case of sympathetic herd-delusion, for in 1692 no less than eleven persons had testified to glimpsing it. There were recent rumours, too, with a baffling and disconcerting amount of agreement. Witnesses said it had long hair and the shape of a rat, but that its sharp-toothed, bearded face was evilly human while its paws were like tiny human hands. It took messages betwixt old Keziah and the devil, and was nursed on the witch's blood—which it sucked like a vampire. Its voice was a kind of loathsome titter, and it could speak all languages. Of all the bizarre monstrosities in Gilman's dreams, nothing filled him with greater panic and nausea than this blasphemous and diminutive hybrid, whose image flitted across his vision in a form a thousandfold more hateful than anything his waking mind had deduced from the ancient records and the modern whispers.

Gilman's dreams consisted largely in plunges through limitless abysses of inexplicably coloured twilight and bafflingly disordered sound; abysses whose material and gravitational properties, and whose relation to his own entity, he could not even begin to explain. He did not walk or climb, fly or swim, crawl or wriggle; yet always experienced a mode of motion partly voluntary and partly involuntary. Of his own condition he could not well judge, for sight of his arms, legs, and torso seemed always cut off by some odd disarrangement of perspective; but he felt that his physical organisation and faculties were somehow marvellously transmuted and obliquely projected—though not without a certain grotesque relationship to his normal proportions and properties.

The abysses were by no means vacant, being crowded with indescribably angled masses of alien-hued substance, some of which appeared to be organic while others seemed inorganic. A few of the organic objects tended to awake vague memories in the back of his mind, though he could form no conscious idea of what they mockingly resembled or suggested. In the later dreams he began to distinguish separate categories into which the organic objects appeared to be divided, and which seemed to involve in each case a radically different species of conduct-pattern and basic motivation. Of these categories one seemed to him to include objects slightly less illogical and irrelevant in their motions than the members of the other categories.

All the objects—organic and inorganic alike—were totally beyond description or even comprehension. Gilman sometimes compared the inorganic masses to prisms, labyrinths, clusters of cubes and planes, and Cyclopean buildings; and the organic things struck him variously as groups of bubbles, octopi, centipedes, living Hindoo idols, and intricate Arabesques roused into a kind of ophidian animation. Everything he saw was unspeakably menacing and horrible; and whenever one of the organic entities appeared by its motions to be noticing him, he felt a stark, hideous fright which generally jolted him awake. Of how the organic entities moved, he could tell no more than of how he moved himself. In time he observed a further mystery—the tendency of certain entities to appear suddenly out of empty space, or to disappear totally with equal suddenness. The shrieking, roaring confusion of sound which permeated the abysses was past all analysis as to pitch, timbre, or rhythm; but seemed to be synchronous with vague visual changes in all the indefinite objects, organic and inorganic alike. Gilman had a constant sense of dread that it might rise to some unbearable degree of intensity during one or another of its obscure, relentlessly inevitable fluctuations.

But it was not in these vortices of complete alienage that he saw Brown Jenkin. That shocking little horror was reserved for certain lighter, sharper dreams which assailed him just before he dropped into the fullest depths of sleep. He would be lying in the dark fighting to keep awake when a faint lambent glow would seem to shimmer around the centuried room, shewing in a violet mist the convergence of angled planes which had seized his brain so insidiously. The horror would appear to pop out of the rat-hole in the corner and patter toward him over the sagging, wide-planked floor with evil expectancy in its tiny, bearded human face—but mercifully, this dream always melted away before the object got close enough to nuzzle him. It had hellishly long, sharp, canine teeth. Gilman tried to stop up the rat-hole every day, but each night the real tenants of the partitions would gnaw away the obstruction, whatever it might be. Once he had the landlord nail tin over it, but the next night the rats gnawed a fresh hole—in making which they pushed or dragged out into the room a curious little fragment of bone.

Gilman did not report his fever to the doctor, for he knew he could not pass the examinations if ordered to the college infirmary when every moment was needed for cramming. As it was, he failed in Calculus D and Advanced General Psychology, though not without hope of making up lost ground before the end of the term. It was in March when the fresh element entered his lighter preliminary dreaming, and the nightmare shape of Brown Jenkin began to be companioned by the nebulous blur which grew more and more to resemble a bent old woman. This addition disturbed him more than he could account for, but finally he decided that it was like an ancient crone whom he had twice actually encountered in the dark tangle of lanes near the abandoned wharves. On those occasions the evil, sardonic, and seemingly unmotivated stare of the beldame had set him almost shivering—especially the first time, when an overgrown rat darting across the shadowed mouth of a neighbouring alley had made him think irrationally of Brown Jenkin. Now, he reflected,

those nervous fears were being mirrored in his disordered dreams.

That the influence of the old house was unwholesome, he could not deny; but traces of his early morbid interest still held him there. He argued that the fever alone was responsible for his nightly phantasies, and that when the touch abated he would be free from the monstrous visions. Those visions, however, were of abhorrent vividness and convincingness, and whenever he awaked he retained a vague sense of having undergone much more than he remembered. He was hideously sure that in unrecalled dreams he had talked with both Brown Jenkin and the old woman, and that they had been urging him to go somewhere with them and to meet a third being of greater potency.

Toward the end of March he began to pick up in his mathematics, though other studies bothered him increasingly. He was getting an intuitive knack for solving Riemannian equations, and astonished Professor Upham by his comprehension of fourth-dimensional and other problems which had floored all the rest of the class. One afternoon there was a discussion of possible freakish curvatures in space, and of theoretical points of approach or even contact between our part of the cosmos and various other regions as distant as the farthest stars or the trans-galactic gulfs themselves—or even as fabulously remote as the tentatively conceivable cosmic units beyond the whole Einsteinian space-time continuum. Gilman's handling of this theme filled everyone with admiration, even though some of his hypothetical illustrations caused an increase in the always plentiful gossip about his nervous and solitary eccentricity. What made the students shake their heads was his sober theory that a man might—given mathematical knowledge admittedly beyond all likelihood of human acquirement—step deliberately from the earth to any other celestial body which might lie at one of an infinity of specific points in the cosmic pattern.

Such a step, he said, would require only two stages; first, a passage out of the three-dimensional sphere we know, and second, a passage back to the three-dimensional sphere at another point, perhaps one of infinite remoteness. That this could be accomplished without loss of life was in many cases conceivable. Any being from any part of three-dimensional space could probably survive in the fourth dimension; and its survival of the second stage would depend upon what alien part of three-dimensional space it might select for its re-entry. Denizens of some planets might be able to live on certain others—even planets belonging to other galaxies, or to similar-dimensional phases of other space-time continua—though of course there must be vast numbers of mutually uninhabitable even though mathematically juxtaposed bodies or zones of space.

It was also possible that the inhabitants of a given dimensional realm could survive entry to many unknown and incomprehensible realms of additional or indefinitely multiplied dimensions—be they within or outside the given space-time continuum—and that the converse would be likewise true. This was a matter for speculation, though one could be fairly certain that the type of mutation involved in a passage from any given dimensional plane to the next higher plane would not be destructive of biological integrity as we understand it. Gilman could not be very clear about his reasons for this last assumption, but his haziness here was more than overbalanced by his clearness on other complex points. Professor Upham especially liked his demonstration of the kinship of higher mathematics to certain phases of magical lore transmitted down the ages from an ineffable antiquity—human or pre-human—whose knowledge of the cosmos and its laws was greater than ours.

Around the first of April Gilman worried considerably because his slow fever did not abate. He was also troubled by what some of his fellow-lodgers said about his sleep-walking. It seemed that he was often absent from his bed, and that the creaking of his floor at certain hours of the night was remarked by the man in the room below. This fellow also spoke of hearing the tread of shod feet in the night; but Gilman was sure he must have been mistaken in this, since shoes as well as other apparel were always precisely in place in the morning. One could develop all sorts of aural delusions in this morbid old house—for did not Gilman himself, even in daylight, now feel certain that noises other than rat-scratchings came from the black voids beyond the slanting wall and above the slanting ceiling? His pathologically sensitive ears began to listen for faint footfalls in the immemorially sealed loft overhead, and sometimes the illusion of such things was agonisingly realistic.

However, he knew that he had actually become a somnambulist; for twice at night his room had been found vacant, though with all his clothing in place. Of this he had been assured by Frank Elwood, the one fellow-student whose poverty forced him to room in this squalid and unpopular house. Elwood had been studying in the small hours and had come up for help on a differential equation, only to find Gilman absent. It had been rather presumptuous of him to open the unlocked door after knocking had failed to rouse a response, but he had needed the help very badly and thought that his host would not mind a gentle prodding awake. On neither occasion, though, had Gilman been there—and when told of the matter he wondered where he could have been wandering, barefoot and with only his night-clothes on. He resolved to investigate the matter if reports of his sleep-walking continued, and thought of sprinkling flour on the floor of the corridor to see where his footsteps might lead. The door was the only conceivable egress, for there was no possible foothold outside the narrow window.

As April advanced Gilman's fever-sharpened ears were disturbed by the whining prayers of a superstitious loom-fixer named Joe Mazurewicz, who had a room on the ground floor. Mazurewicz had told long, rambling stories about the ghost of old Keziah and the furry, sharp-fanged, nuzzling thing, and had said he was so badly haunted at times that only his silver crucifix—given him for the purpose by Father Iwanicki of St. Stanislaus' Church—could bring him relief. Now he was praying because the Witches' Sabbath was drawing near. May-Eve was Walpurgis-Night, when hell's blackest evil roamed the earth and all the slaves of Satan gathered for nameless rites and deeds. It was always a very bad time in Arkham, even though the fine folks up in Miskatonic Avenue and High and Saltonstall Streets pretended to know nothing about it. There would be bad doings—and a child or two would probably be missing. Joe knew about such things, for his grandmother in the old country had heard tales from her grandmother. It was wise to pray and count one's beads at this season. For three months Keziah and Brown Jenkin had not been near Joe's room, nor near Paul Choynski's room, nor anywhere else—and it meant no good when they held off like that. They must be up to something.

Gilman dropped in at a doctor's office on the 16th of the month, and was surprised to find his temperature was not as high as he had feared. The physician questioned him sharply, and advised him to see a nerve specialist. On reflection, he was glad he had not consulted the still more inquisitive college doctor. Old Waldron, who had curtailed his activities before, would have made him take a rest—an impossible thing now that he was so close to great results in his equations. He was certainly near the boundary between the known universe and the fourth dimension, and who could say how much farther he might go?

But even as these thoughts came to him he wondered at the source of his strange confidence. Did all of this perilous sense of imminence come from the formulae on the sheets he covered day by day? The soft, stealthy, imaginary footsteps in the sealed loft above were unnerving. And now, too, there was a growing feeling that somebody was constantly persuading him to do something terrible which he could not do. How about the somnambulism? Where did he go sometimes in the night? And what was that faint suggestion of sound which once in a while seemed to trickle through the maddening confusion of identifiable sounds even in broad daylight and full wakefulness? Its rhythm did not correspond to anything on earth, unless perhaps to the cadence of one or two unmentionable Sabbat-chants, and sometimes he feared it corresponded to certain attributes of the vague shrieking or roaring in those wholly alien abysses of dream.

The dreams were meanwhile getting to be atrocious. In the lighter preliminary phase the evil old woman was now of fiendish distinctness, and Gilman knew she was the one who had frightened him in the slums. Her bent back, long nose, and shrivelled chin were unmistakable, and her shapeless brown garments were like those he remembered. The expression on her face was one of hideous malevolence and exultation, and when he awaked he could recall a croaking voice that persuaded and threatened. He must meet the

Black Man, and go with them all to the throne of Azathoth at the centre of ultimate Chaos. That was what she said. He must sign in his own blood the book of Azathoth and take a new secret name now that his independent delvings had gone so far. What kept him from going with her and Brown Jenkin and the other to the throne of Chaos where the thin flutes pipe mindlessly was the fact that he had seen the name "Azathoth" in the Necronomicon, and knew it stood for a primal evil too horrible for description.

The old woman always appeared out of thin air near the corner where the downward slant met the inward slant. She seemed to crystallise at a point closer to the ceiling than to the floor, and every night she was a little nearer and more distinct before the dream shifted. Brown Jenkin, too, was always a little nearer at the last, and its yellowish-white fangs glistened shockingly in that unearthly violet phosphorescence. Its shrill loathsome tittering stuck more and more in Gilman's head, and he could remember in the morning how it had pronounced the words "Azathoth" and "Nyarlathotep".

In the deeper dreams everything was likewise more distinct, and Gilman felt that the twilight abysses around him were those of the fourth dimension. Those organic entities whose motions seemed least flagrantly irrelevant and unmotivated were probably projections of life-forms from our own planet, including human beings. What the others were in their own dimensional sphere or spheres he dared not try to think. Two of the less irrelevantly moving things—a rather large congeries of iridescent, prolately spheroidal bubbles and a very much smaller polyhedron of unknown colours and rapidly shifting surface angles—seemed to take notice of him and follow him about or float ahead as he changed position among the titan prisms, labyrinths, cube-and-plane clusters, and quasi-buildings; and all the while the vague shrieking and roaring waxed louder and louder, as if approaching some monstrous climax of utterly unendurable intensity.

During the night of April 19–20 the new development occurred. Gilman was half-involuntarily moving about in the twilight abysses with the bubble-mass and the small polyhedron floating ahead, when he noticed the peculiarly regular angles formed by the edges of some gigantic neighbouring prism-clusters. In another second he was out of the abyss and standing tremulously on a rocky hillside bathed in intense, diffused green light. He was barefooted and in his night-clothes, and when he tried to walk discovered that he could scarcely lift his feet. A swirling vapour hid everything but the immediate sloping terrain from sight, and he shrank from the thought of the sounds that might surge out of that vapour.

Then he saw the two shapes laboriously crawling toward him—the old woman and the little furry thing. The crone strained up to her knees and managed to cross her arms in a singular fashion, while Brown Jenkin pointed in a certain direction with a horribly anthropoid fore paw which it raised with evident difficulty. Spurred by an impulse he did not originate, Gilman dragged himself forward along a course determined by the angle of the old woman's arms and the direction of the small monstrosity's paw, and before he had shuffled three steps he was back in the twilight abysses. Geometrical shapes seethed around him, and he fell dizzily and interminably. At last he woke in his bed in the crazily angled garret of the eldritch old house.

He was good for nothing that morning, and stayed away from all his classes. Some unknown attraction was pulling his eyes in a seemingly irrelevant direction, for he could not help staring at a certain vacant spot on the floor. As the day advanced the focus of his unseeing eyes changed position, and by noon he had conquered the impulse to stare at vacancy. About two o'clock he went out for lunch, and as he threaded the narrow lanes of the city he found himself turning always to the southeast. Only an effort halted him at a cafeteria in Church Street, and after the meal he felt the unknown pull still more strongly.

He would have to consult a nerve specialist after all—perhaps there was a connexion with his somnambulism—but meanwhile he might at least try to break the morbid spell himself. Undoubtedly he could still manage to walk away from the pull; so with great resolution he headed against it and dragged himself deliberately north along Garrison Street. By the time he had reached the bridge over the Miskatonic he was in a cold perspiration, and he clutched at the iron railing as he gazed upstream at the ill-regarded island whose regular lines of ancient standing stones brooded sullenly in the afternoon sunlight.

Then he gave a start. For there was a clearly visible living figure on that desolate island, and a second glance told him it was certainly the strange old woman whose sinister aspect had worked itself so disastrously into his dreams. The tall grass near her was moving, too, as if some other living thing were crawling close to the ground. When the old woman began to turn toward him he fled precipitately off the bridge and into the shelter of the town's labyrinthine waterfront alleys. Distant though the island was, he felt that a monstrous and invincible evil could flow from the sardonic stare of that bent, ancient figure in brown.

The southeastward pull still held, and only with tremendous resolution could Gilman drag himself into the old house and up the rickety stairs. For hours he sat silent and aimless, with his eyes shifting gradually westward. About six o'clock his sharpened ears caught the whining prayers of Joe Mazurewicz two floors below, and in desperation he seized his hat and walked out into the sunset-golden streets, letting the now directly southward pull carry him where it might. An hour later darkness found him in the open fields beyond Hangman's Brook, with the glimmering spring stars shining ahead. The urge to walk was gradually changing to an urge to leap mystically into space, and suddenly he realised just where the source of the pull lay.

It was in the sky. A definite point among the stars had a claim on him and was calling him. Apparently it was a point somewhere between Hydra and Argo Navis, and he knew that he had been urged toward it ever since he had awaked soon after dawn. In the morning it had been underfoot; afternoon found it rising in the southeast, and now it was roughly south but wheeling toward the west. What was the meaning of this new thing? Was he going mad? How long would it last? Again mustering his resolution, Gilman turned and dragged himself back to the sinister old house.

Mazurewicz was waiting for him at the door, and seemed both anxious and reluctant to whisper some fresh bit of superstition. It was about the witch light. Joe had been out celebrating the night before—it was Patriots' Day in Massachusetts—and had come home after midnight. Looking up at the house from outside, he had thought at first that Gilman's window was dark; but then he had seen the faint violet glow within. He wanted to warn the gentleman about that glow, for everybody in Arkham knew it was Keziah's witch light which played near Brown Jenkin and the ghost of the old crone herself. He had not mentioned this before, but now he must tell about it because it meant that Keziah and her long-toothed familiar were haunting the young gentleman. Sometimes he and Paul Choynski and Landlord Dombrowski thought they saw that light seeping out of cracks in the sealed loft above the young gentleman's room, but they had all agreed not to talk about that. However, it would be better for the gentleman to take another room and get a crucifix from some good priest like Father Iwanicki.

As the man rambled on Gilman felt a nameless panic clutch at his throat. He knew that Joe must have been half drunk when he came home the night before, yet this mention of a violet light in the garret window was of frightful import. It was a lambent glow of this sort which always played about the old woman and the small furry thing in those lighter, sharper dreams which prefaced his plunge into unknown abysses, and the thought that a wakeful second person could see the dream-luminance was utterly beyond sane harbourage. Yet where had the fellow got such an odd notion? Had he himself talked as well as walked around the house in his sleep? No, Joe said, he had not—but he must check up on this. Perhaps Frank Elwood could tell him something, though he hated to ask.

Fever—wilddreams—somnambulism—illusions of sounds—a pull toward a point in the sky—and now a suspicion of insane sleep-talking! He must stop studying, see a nerve specialist, and take himself in hand. When he climbed to the second story he paused at Elwood's door but saw that the other youth was out. Reluctantly he continued up to his garret room and sat down in the dark. His gaze was still pulled to the southwest, but he also found himself listening intently for some sound in the closed loft above, and half imagining that an evil violet light seeped down through an infinitesimal crack in the low, slanting ceiling.

That night as Gilman slept the violet light broke upon him with heightened intensity, and the old witch and small furry thing—getting closer than ever before—mocked him with inhuman squeals and devilish gestures. He was glad to sink into the vaguely roaring twilight abysses, though the pursuit of that iridescent bubble-congeries and that kaleidoscopic little polyhedron was menacing and irritating. Then came the shift as vast converging planes of a slippery-looking substance loomed above and below him—a shift which ended in a flash of delirium and a blaze of unknown, alien light in which yellow, carmine, and indigo were madly and inextricably blended.

He was half lying on a high, fantastically balustraded terrace above a boundless jungle of outlandish, incredible peaks, balanced planes, domes, minarets, horizontal discs poised on pinnacles, and numberless forms of still greater wildness—some of stone and some of metal—which glittered gorgeously in the mixed, almost blistering glare from a polychromatic sky. Looking upward he saw three stupendous discs of flame, each of a different hue, and at a different height above an infinitely distant curving horizon of low mountains. Behind him tiers of higher terraces towered aloft as far as he could see. The city below stretched away to the limits of vision, and he hoped that no sound would well up from it.

The pavement from which he easily raised himself was of a veined, polished stone beyond his power to identify, and the tiles were cut in bizarre-angled shapes which struck him as less asymmetrical than based on some unearthly symmetry whose laws he could not comprehend. The balustrade was chest-high, delicate, and fantastically wrought, while along the rail were ranged at short intervals little figures of grotesque design and exquisite workmanship. They, like the whole balustrade, seemed to be made of some sort of shining metal whose colour could not be guessed in this chaos of mixed effulgences; and their nature utterly defied conjecture. They represented some ridged, barrel-shaped object with thin horizontal arms radiating spoke-like from a central ring, and with vertical knobs or bulbs projecting from the head and base of the barrel. Each of these knobs was the hub of a system of five long, flat, triangularly tapering arms arranged around it like the arms of a starfish—nearly horizontal, but curving slightly away from the central barrel. The base of the bottom knob was fused to the long railing with so delicate a point of contact that several figures had been broken off and were missing. The figures were about four and a half inches in height, while the spiky arms gave them a maximum diameter of about two and a half inches.

When Gilman stood up the tiles felt hot to his bare feet. He was wholly alone, and his first act was to walk to the balustrade and look dizzily down at the endless, Cyclopean city almost two thousand feet below. As he listened he thought a rhythmic confusion of faint musical pipings covering a wide tonal range welled up from the narrow streets beneath, and he wished he might discern the denizens of the place. The sight turned him giddy after a while, so that he would have fallen to the pavement had he not clutched instinctively at the lustrous balustrade. His right hand fell on one of the projecting figures, the touch seeming to steady him slightly. It was too much, however, for the exotic delicacy of the metal-work, and the spiky figure snapped off under his grasp. Still half-dazed, he continued to clutch it as his other hand seized a vacant space on the smooth railing.

But now his oversensitive ears caught something behind him, and he looked back across the level terrace. Approaching him softly though without apparent furtiveness were five figures, two of which were the sinister old woman and the fanged, furry little animal. The other three were what sent him unconscious—for they were living entities about eight feet high, shaped precisely like the spiky images on the balustrade, and propelling themselves by a spider-like wriggling of their lower set of starfish-arms.

Gilman awakened in his bed, drenched by a cold perspiration and with a smarting sensation in his face, hands, and feet. Springing to the floor, he washed and dressed in frantic haste, as if it were necessary for him to get out of the house as quickly as possible. He did not know where he wished to go, but felt that once more he would have to sacrifice his classes. The odd pull toward that spot in the sky between Hydra and Argo had abated, but another of even greater strength had taken its place. Now he felt that he must go north—infinitely north. He dreaded to cross the bridge that gave a view of the desolate island in the Miskatonic, so went over the Peabody Avenue bridge. Very often he stumbled, for his eyes and ears were chained to an extremely lofty point in the blank blue sky.

After about an hour he got himself under better control, and saw that he was far from the city. All around him stretched the bleak emptiness of salt marshes, while the narrow road ahead led to Innsmouth—that ancient, half-deserted town which Arkham people were so curiously unwilling to visit. Though the northward pull had not diminished, he resisted it as he had resisted the other pull, and finally found that he could almost balance the one against the other. Plodding back to town and getting some coffee at a soda fountain, he dragged himself into the public library and browsed aimlessly among the lighter magazines. Once he met some friends who remarked how oddly sunburned he looked, but he did not tell them of his walk. At three o'clock he took some lunch at a restaurant, noting meanwhile that the pull had either lessened or divided itself. After that he killed the time at a cheap cinema show, seeing the inane performance over and over again without paying any attention to it.

About nine at night he drifted homeward and stumbled into the ancient house. Joe Mazurewicz was whining unintelligible prayers, and Gilman hastened up to his own garret chamber without pausing to see if Elwood was in. It was when he turned on the feeble electric light that the shock came. At once he saw there was something on the table which did not belong there, and a second look left no room for doubt. Lying on its side—for it could not stand up alone—was the exotic spiky figure which in his monstrous dream he had broken off the fantastic balustrade. No detail was missing. The ridged, barrel-shaped centre, the thin, radiating arms, the knobs at each end, and the flat, slightly outward-curving starfish-arms spreading from those knobs—all were there. In the electric light the colour seemed to be a kind of iridescent grey veined with green, and Gilman could see amidst his horror and bewilderment that one of the knobs ended in a jagged break corresponding to its former point of attachment to the dream-railing.

Only his tendency toward a dazed stupor prevented him from screaming aloud. This fusion of dream and reality was too much to bear. Still dazed, he clutched at the spiky thing and staggered downstairs to Landlord Dombrowski's quarters. The whining prayers of the superstitious loomfixer were still sounding through the mouldy halls, but Gilman did not mind them now. The landlord was in, and greeted him pleasantly. No, he had not seen that thing before and did not know anything about it. But his wife had said she found a funny tin thing in one of the beds when she fixed the rooms at noon, and maybe that was it. Dombrowski called her, and she waddled in. Yes, that was the thing. She had found it in the young gentleman's bed—on the side next the wall. It had looked very queer to her, but of course the young gentleman had lots of queer things in his room—books and curios and pictures and markings on paper. She certainly knew nothing about it.

So Gilman climbed upstairs again in a mental turmoil, convinced that he was either still dreaming or that his somnambulism had run to incredible extremes and led him to depredations in unknown places. Where had he got this outré thing? He did not recall seeing it in any museum in Arkham. It must have been somewhere, though; and the sight of it as he snatched it in his sleep must have caused the odd dream-picture of the balustraded terrace. Next day he would make some very guarded inquiries—and perhaps see the nerve specialist.

Meanwhile he would try to keep track of his somnambulism. As he went upstairs and across the garret hall he sprinkled about some flour which he had borrowed—with a frank admission as to its purpose—from the landlord. He had stopped at Elwood's door on the way, but had found all dark within. Entering his room, he placed the spiky thing on the table, and lay down in complete mental and physical exhaustion without pausing to undress. From the closed loft above the slanting ceiling he thought he heard a faint scratching and padding, but he was too disorganised even to mind it. That cryptical pull from the north was getting very strong again, though it seemed now to come from a lower place in the sky.

In the dazzling violet light of dream the old woman and the fanged, furry thing came again and with a greater distinctness than on any former occasion.

This time they actually reached him, and he felt the crone's withered claws clutching at him. He was pulled out of bed and into empty space, and for a moment he heard a rhythmic roaring and saw the twilight amorphousness of the vague abysses seething around him. But that moment was very brief, for presently he was in a crude, windowless little space with rough beams and planks rising to a peak just above his head, and with a curious slanting floor underfoot. Propped level on that floor were low cases full of books of every degree of antiquity and disintegration, and in the centre were a table and bench, both apparently fastened in place. Small objects of unknown shape and nature were ranged on the tops of the cases, and in the flaming violet light Gilman thought he saw a counterpart of the spiky image which had puzzled him so horribly. On the left the floor fell abruptly away, leaving a black triangular gulf out of which, after a second's dry rattling, there presently climbed the hateful little furry thing with the yellow fangs and bearded human face.

The evilly grinning beldame still clutched him, and beyond the table stood a figure he had never seen before—a tall, lean man of dead black colouration but without the slightest sign of negroid features; wholly devoid of either hair or beard, and wearing as his only garment a shapeless robe of some heavy black fabric. His feet were indistinguishable because of the table and bench, but he must have been shod, since there was a clicking whenever he changed position. The man did not speak, and bore no trace of expression on his small, regular features. He merely pointed to a book of prodigious size which lay open on the table, while the beldame thrust a huge grey quill into Gilman's right hand. Over everything was a pall of intensely maddening fear, and the climax was reached when the furry thing ran up the dreamer's clothing to his shoulders and then down his left arm, finally biting him sharply in the wrist just below his cuff. As the blood spurted from this wound Gilman lapsed into a faint.

He awaked on the morning of the 22nd with a pain in his left wrist, and saw that his cuff was brown with dried blood. His recollections were very confused, but the scene with the black man in the unknown space stood out vividly. The rats must have bitten him as he slept, giving rise to the climax of that frightful dream. Opening the door, he saw that the flour on the corridor floor was undisturbed except for the huge prints of the loutish fellow who roomed at the other end of the garret. So he had not been sleep-walking this time. But something would have to be done about those rats. He would speak to the landlord about them. Again he tried to stop up the hole at the base of the slanting wall, wedging in a candlestick which seemed of about the right size. His ears were ringing horribly, as if with the residual echoes of some horrible noise heard in dreams.

As he bathed and changed clothes he tried to recall what he had dreamed after the scene in the violet-litten space, but nothing definite would crystallise in his mind. That scene itself must have corresponded to the sealed loft overhead, which had begun to attack his imagination so violently, but later impressions were faint and hazy. There were suggestions of the vague, twilight abysses, and of still vaster, blacker abysses beyond them—abysses in which all fixed suggestions of form were absent. He had been taken there by the bubble-congeries and the little polyhedron which always dogged him; but they, like himself, had changed to wisps of milky, barely luminous mist in this farther void of ultimate blackness. Something else had gone on ahead—a larger wisp which now and then condensed into nameless approximations of form—and he thought that their progress had not been in a straight line, but rather along the alien curves and spirals of some ethereal vortex which obeyed laws unknown to the physics and mathematics of any conceivable cosmos. Eventually there had been a hint of vast, leaping shadows, of a monstrous, half-acoustic pulsing, and of the thin, monotonous piping of an unseen flute—but that was all. Gilman decided he had picked up that last conception from what he had read in the Necronomicon about the mindless entity Azathoth, which rules all time and space from a curiously environed black throne at the centre of Chaos.

When the blood was washed away the wrist wound proved very slight, and Gilman puzzled over the location of the two tiny punctures. It occurred to him that there was no blood on the bedspread where he had lain—which was very curious in view of the amount on his skin and cuff. Had he been sleep-walking within his room, and had the rat bitten him as he sat in some chair or paused in some less rational position? He looked in every corner for brownish drops or stains, but did not find any. He had better, he thought, sprinkle flour within the room as well as outside the door—though after all no further proof of his sleep-walking was needed. He knew he did walk—and the thing to do now was to stop it. He must ask Frank Elwood for help. This morning the strange pulls from space seemed lessened, though they were replaced by another sensation even more inexplicable. It was a vague, insistent impulse to fly away from his present situation, but held not a hint of the specific direction in which he wished to fly. As he picked up the strange spiky image on the table he thought the older northward pull grew a trifle stronger; but even so, it was wholly overruled by the newer and more bewildering urge.

He took the spiky image down to Elwood's room, steeling himself against the whines of the loomfixer which welled up from the ground floor. Elwood was in, thank heaven, and appeared to be stirring about. There was time for a little conversation before leaving for breakfast and college, so Gilman hurriedly poured forth an account of his recent dreams and fears. His host was very sympathetic, and agreed that something ought to be done. He was shocked by his guest's drawn, haggard aspect, and noticed the queer, abnormal-looking sunburn which others had remarked during the past week. There was not much, though, that he could say. He had not seen Gilman on any sleep-walking expedition, and had no idea what the curious image could be. He had, though, heard the French-Canadian who lodged just under Gilman talking to Mazurewicz one evening. They were telling each other how badly they dreaded the coming of Walpurgis-Night, now only a few days off; and were exchanging pitying comments about the poor, doomed young gentleman. Desrochers, the fellow under Gilman's room, had spoken of nocturnal footsteps both shod and unshod, and of the violet light he saw one night when he had stolen fearfully up to peer through Gilman's keyhole. He had not dared to peer, he told Mazurewicz, after he had glimpsed that light through the cracks around the door. There had been soft talking, too—and as he began to describe it his voice had sunk to an inaudible whisper.

Elwood could not imagine what had set these superstitious creatures gossiping, but supposed their imaginations had been roused by Gilman's late hours and somnolent walking and talking on the one hand, and by the nearness of traditionally feared May-Eve on the other hand. That Gilman talked in his sleep was plain, and it was obviously from Desrochers' keyhole-listenings that the delusive notion of the violet dream-light had got abroad. These simple people were quick to imagine they had seen any odd thing they had heard about. As for a plan of action—Gilman had better move down to Elwood's room and avoid sleeping alone. Elwood would, if awake, rouse him whenever he began to talk or rise in his sleep. Very soon, too, he must see the specialist. Meanwhile they would take the spiky image around to the various museums and to certain professors; seeking identification and stating that it had been found in a public rubbish-can. Also, Dombrowski must attend to the poisoning of those rats in the walls.

Braced up by Elwood's companionship, Gilman attended classes that day. Strange urges still tugged at him, but he could sidetrack them with considerable success. During a free period he shewed the queer image to several professors, all of whom were intensely interested, though none of them could shed any light upon its nature or origin. That night he slept on a couch which Elwood had had the landlord bring to the second-story room, and for the first time in weeks was wholly free from disquieting dreams. But the feverishness still hung on, and the whines of the loomfixer were an unnerving influence.

During the next few days Gilman enjoyed an almost perfect immunity from morbid manifestations. He had, Elwood said, shewed no tendency to talk or rise in his sleep; and meanwhile the landlord was putting rat-poison everywhere. The only disturbing element was the talk among the superstitious foreigners, whose imaginations had become highly excited. Mazurewicz was always trying to make him get a crucifix, and finally forced one upon him which he said had been blessed by the good Father Iwanicki. Desrochers, too, had something to say—in fact, he insisted that cautious steps had sounded in the now vacant room above him on the first and second nights of Gilman's absence from it. Paul Choynski thought he heard sounds in the halls and on the stairs at night, and claimed that his door had been softly tried, while Mrs. Dombrowski vowed she had seen Brown Jenkin for the first time since All-Hallows. But such naive reports could mean very little, and Gilman let the cheap metal crucifix hang idly from a knob on his host's dresser.

For three days Gilman and Elwood canvassed the local museums in an effort to identify the strange spiky image, but always without success. In every quarter, however, interest was intense; for the utter alienage of the thing was a tremendous challenge to scientific curiosity. One of the small radiating arms was broken off and subjected to chemical analysis, and the result is still talked about in college circles. Professor Ellery found platinum, iron, and tellurium in the strange alloy; but mixed with these were at least three other apparent elements of high atomic weight which chemistry was absolutely powerless to classify. Not only did they fail to correspond with any known element, but they did not even fit the vacant places reserved for probable elements in the periodic system. The mystery remains unsolved to this day, though the image is on exhibition at the museum of Miskatonic University.

On the morning of April 27 a fresh rat-hole appeared in the room where Gilman was a guest, but Dombrowski tinned it up during the day. The poison was not having much effect, for scratchings and scurryings in the walls were virtually undiminished. Elwood was out late that night, and Gilman waited up for him. He did not wish to go to sleep in a room alone—especially since he thought he had glimpsed in the evening twilight the repellent old woman whose image had become so horribly transferred to his dreams. He wondered who she was, and what had been near her rattling the tin can in a rubbish-heap at the mouth of a squalid courtyard. The crone had seemed to notice him and leer evilly at him—though perhaps this was merely his imagination.

The next day both youths felt very tired, and knew they would sleep like logs when night came. In the evening they drowsily discussed the mathematical studies which had so completely and perhaps harmfully engrossed Gilman, and speculated about the linkage with ancient magic and folklore which seemed so darkly probable. They spoke of old Keziah Mason, and Elwood agreed that Gilman had good scientific grounds for thinking she might have stumbled on strange and significant information. The hidden cults to which these witches belonged often guarded and handed down surprising secrets from elder, forgotten aeons; and it was by no means impossible that Keziah had actually mastered the art of passing through dimensional gates. Tradition emphasises the uselessness of material barriers in halting a witch's motions; and who can say what underlies the old tales of broomstick rides through the night?

Whether a modern student could ever gain similar powers from mathematical research alone, was still to be seen. Success, Gilman added, might lead to dangerous and unthinkable situations; for who could foretell the conditions pervading an adjacent but normally inaccessible dimension? On the other hand, the picturesque possibilities were enormous. Time could not exist in certain belts of space, and by entering and remaining in such a belt one might preserve one's life and age indefinitely; never suffering organic metabolism or deterioration except for slight amounts incurred during visits to one's own or similar planes. One might, for example, pass into a timeless dimension and emerge at some remote period of the earth's history as young as before.

Whether anybody had ever managed to do this, one could hardly conjecture with any degree of authority. Old legends are hazy and ambiguous, and in historic times all attempts at crossing forbidden gaps seem complicated by strange and terrible alliances with beings and messengers from outside. There was the immemorial figure of the deputy or messenger of hidden and terrible powers—the "Black Man" of the witch-cult, and the "Nyarlathotep" of the Necronomicon. There was, too, the baffling problem of the lesser messengers or intermediaries—the quasi-animals and queer hybrids which legend depicts as witches' familiars. As Gilman and Elwood retired, too sleepy to argue further, they heard Joe Mazurewicz reel into the house half-drunk, and shuddered at the desperate wildness of his whining prayers.

That night Gilman saw the violet light again. In his dream he had heard a scratching and gnawing in the partitions, and thought that someone fumbled clumsily at the latch. Then he saw the old woman and the small furry thing advancing toward him over the carpeted floor. The beldame's face was alight with inhuman exultation, and the little yellow-toothed morbidity tittered mockingly as it pointed at the heavily sleeping form of Elwood on the other couch across the room. A paralysis of fear stifled all attempts to cry out. As once before, the hideous crone seized Gilman by the shoulders, yanking him out of bed and into empty space. Again the infinitude of the shrieking twilight abysses flashed past him, but in another second he thought he was in a dark, muddy, unknown alley of foetid odours, with the rotting walls of ancient houses towering up on every hand.

Ahead was the robed black man he had seen in the peaked space in the other dream, while from a lesser distance the old woman was beckoning and grimacing imperiously. Brown Jenkin was rubbing itself with a kind of affectionate playfulness around the ankles of the black man, which the deep mud largely concealed. There was a dark open doorway on the right, to which the black man silently pointed. Into this the grimacing crone started, dragging Gilman after her by his pajama sleeve. There were evil-smelling staircases which creaked ominously, and on which the old woman seemed to radiate a faint violet light; and finally a door leading off a landing. The crone fumbled with the latch and pushed the door open, motioning to Gilman to wait and disappearing inside the black aperture.

The youth's oversensitive ears caught a hideous strangled cry, and presently the beldame came out of the room bearing a small, senseless form which she thrust at the dreamer as if ordering him to carry it. The sight of this form, and the expression on its face, broke the spell. Still too dazed to cry out, he plunged recklessly down the noisome staircase and into the mud outside; halting only when seized and choked by the waiting black man. As consciousness departed he heard the faint, shrill tittering of the fanged, rat-like abnormality.

On the morning of the 29th Gilman awaked into a maelstrom of horror. The instant he opened his eyes he knew something was terribly wrong, for he was back in his old garret room with the slanting wall and ceiling, sprawled on the now unmade bed. His throat was aching inexplicably, and as he struggled to a sitting posture he saw with growing fright that his feet and pajama-bottoms were brown with caked mud. For the moment his recollections were hopelessly hazy, but he knew at least that he must have been sleep-walking. Elwood had been lost too deeply in slumber to hear and stop him. On the floor were confused muddy prints, but oddly enough they did not extend all the way to the door. The more Gilman looked at them, the more peculiar they

seemed; for in addition to those he could recognise as his there were some smaller, almost round markings—such as the legs of a large chair or table might make, except that most of them tended to be divided into halves. There were also some curious muddy rat-tracks leading out of a fresh hole and back into it again. Utter bewilderment and the fear of madness racked Gilman as he staggered to the door and saw that there were no muddy prints outside. The more he remembered of his hideous dream the more terrified he felt, and it added to his desperation to hear Joe Mazurewicz chanting mournfully two floors below.

Descending to Elwood's room he roused his still-sleeping host and began telling of how he had found himself, but Elwood could form no idea of what might really have happened. Where Gilman could have been, how he got back to his room without making tracks in the hall, and how the muddy, furniture-like prints came to be mixed with his in the garret chamber, were wholly beyond conjecture. Then there were those dark, livid marks on his throat, as if he had tried to strangle himself. He put his hands up to them, but found that they did not even approximately fit. While they were talking Desrochers dropped in to say that he had heard a terrific clattering overhead in the dark small hours. No, there had been no one on the stairs after midnight—though just before midnight he had heard faint footfalls in the garret, and cautiously descending steps he did not like. It was, he added, a very bad time of year for Arkham. The young gentleman had better be sure to wear the crucifix Joe Mazurewicz had given him. Even the daytime was not safe, for after dawn there had been strange sounds in the house—especially a thin, childish wail hastily choked off.

Gilman mechanically attended classes that morning, but was wholly unable to fix his mind on his studies. A mood of hideous apprehension and expectancy had seized him, and he seemed to be awaiting the fall of some annihilating blow. At noon he lunched at the University Spa, picking up a paper from the next seat as he waited for dessert. But he never ate that dessert; for an item on the paper's first page left him limp, wild-eyed, and able only to pay his check and stagger back to Elwood's room.

There had been a strange kidnapping the night before in Orne's Gangway, and the two-year-old child of a clod-like laundry worker named Anastasia Wolejko had completely vanished from sight. The mother, it appeared, had feared the event for some time; but the reasons she assigned for her fear were so grotesque that no one took them seriously. She had, she said, seen Brown Jenkin about the place now and then ever since early in March, and knew from its grimaces and titterings that little Ladislas must be marked for sacrifice at the awful Sabbat on Walpurgis-Night. She had asked her neighbour Mary Czanek to sleep in the room and try to protect the child, but Mary had not dared. She could not tell the police, for they never believed such things. Children had been taken that way every year ever since she could remember. And her friend Pete Stowacki would not help because he wanted the child out of the way anyhow.

But what threw Gilman into a cold perspiration was the report of a pair of revellers who had been walking past the mouth of the gangway just after midnight. They admitted they had been drunk, but both vowed they had seen a crazily dressed trio furtively entering the dark passageway. There had, they said, been a huge robed negro, a little old woman in rags, and a young white man in his night-clothes. The old woman had been dragging the youth, while around the feet of the negro a tame rat was rubbing and weaving in the brown mud.

Gilman sat in a daze all the afternoon, and Elwood—who had meanwhile seen the papers and formed terrible conjectures from them—found him thus when he came home. This time neither could doubt but that something hideously serious was closing in around them. Between the phantasms of nightmare and the realities of the objective world a monstrous and unthinkable relationship was crystallising, and only stupendous vigilance could avert still more direful developments. Gilman must see a specialist sooner or later, but not just now, when all the papers were full of this kidnapping business.

Just what had really happened was maddeningly obscure, and for a moment both Gilman and Elwood exchanged whispered theories of the wildest kind. Had Gilman unconsciously succeeded better than he knew in his studies of space and its dimensions? Had he actually slipped outside our sphere to points unguessed and unimaginable? Where—if anywhere—had he been on those nights of daemoniac alienage? The roaring twilight abysses—the green hillside—the blistering terrace—the pulls from the stars—the ultimate black vortex—the black man—the muddy alley and the stairs—the old witch and the fanged, furry horror—the bubble-congeries and the little polyhedron—the strange sunburn—the wrist wound—the unexplained image—the muddy feet—the throat-marks—the tales and fears of the superstitious foreigners—what did all this mean? To what extent could the laws of sanity apply to such a case?

There was no sleep for either of them that night, but next day they both cut classes and drowsed. This was April 30th, and with the dusk would come the hellish Sabbat-time which all the foreigners and the superstitious old folk feared.

Mazurewicz came home at six o'clock and said people at the mill were whispering that the Walpurgis-revels would be held in the dark ravine beyond Meadow Hill where the old white stone stands in a place queerly void of all plant-life. Some of them had even told the police and advised them to look there for the missing Wolejko child, but they did not believe anything would be done. Joe insisted that the poor young gentleman wear his nickel-chained crucifix, and Gilman put it on and dropped it inside his shirt to humour the fellow.

Late at night the two youths sat drowsing in their chairs, lulled by the rhythmical praying of the loomfixer on the floor below. Gilman listened as he nodded, his preternaturally sharpened hearing seeming to strain for some subtle, dreaded murmur beyond the noises in the ancient house. Unwholesome recollections of things in the Necronomicon and the Black Book welled up, and he found himself swaying to infandous rhythms said to pertain to the blackest ceremonies of the Sabbat and to have an origin outside the time and space we comprehend.

Presently he realised what he was listening for—the hellish chant of the celebrants in the distant black valley. How did he know so much about what they expected? How did he know the time when Nahab and her acolyte were due to bear the brimming bowl which would follow the black cock and the black goat? He saw that Elwood had dropped asleep, and tried to call out and waken him. Something, however, closed his throat. He was not his own master. Had he signed the black man's book after all?

Then his fevered, abnormal hearing caught the distant, windborne notes. Over miles of hill and field and alley they came, but he recognised them none the less. The fires must be lit, and the dancers must be starting in. How could he keep himself from going? What was it that had enmeshed him? Mathematics—folklore—the house—old Keziah—Brown Jenkin . . . and now he saw that there was a fresh rat-hole in the wall near his couch. Above the distant chanting and the nearer praying of Joe Mazurewicz came another sound—a stealthy, determined scratching in the partitions. He hoped the electric lights would not go out. Then he saw the fanged, bearded little face in the rat-hole—the accursed little face which he at last realised bore such a shocking, mocking resemblance to old Keziah's—and heard the faint fumbling at the door.

The screaming twilight abysses flashed before him, and he felt himself helpless in the formless grasp of the iridescent bubble-congeries. Ahead raced the small, kaleidoscopic polyhedron, and all through the churning void there was a heightening and acceleration of the vague tonal pattern which seemed to foreshadow some unutterable and unendurable climax. He seemed to know what was coming—the monstrous burst of Walpurgis-rhythm in whose cosmic timbre would be concentrated all the primal, ultimate space-time seethings which lie behind the massed spheres of matter and sometimes break forth in measured reverberations that penetrate faintly to every layer of entity and give hideous significance throughout the worlds to certain dreaded periods.

But all this vanished in a second. He was again in the cramped, violet-litten peaked space with the slanting floor, the low cases of ancient books, the bench and table, the queer objects, and the triangular gulf at one side. On the table lay a small white figure—an infant boy, unclothed and unconscious—while on the other side stood the monstrous, leering old woman with a gleaming, grotesque-hafted knife in her right hand, and a queerly proportioned pale metal bowl covered with curiously chased designs and having delicate lateral handles in her left. She was intoning some croaking ritual in a language which Gilman could not understand, but which seemed like something guardedly quoted in the Necronomicon.

As the scene grew clear he saw the ancient crone bend forward and extend the empty bowl across the table—and unable to control his own motions, he reached far forward and took it in both hands, noticing as he did so its comparative lightness. At the same moment the disgusting form of Brown Jenkin scrambled up over the brink of the triangular black gulf on his left. The crone now motioned him to hold the bowl in a certain position while she raised the huge, grotesque knife above the small white victim as high as her right hand could reach. The fanged, furry thing began tittering a continuation of the unknown ritual, while the witch croaked loathsome responses. Gilman felt a gnawing, poignant abhorrence shoot through his mental and emotional paralysis, and the light metal bowl shook in his grasp. A second later the downward motion of the knife broke the spell completely, and he dropped the bowl with a resounding bell-like clangour while his hands darted out frantically to stop the monstrous deed.

In an instant he had edged up the slanting floor around the end of the table and wrenched the knife from the old woman's claws; sending it clattering over the brink of the narrow triangular gulf. In another instant, however, matters were reversed; for those murderous claws had locked themselves tightly around his own throat, while the wrinkled face was twisted with insane fury. He felt the chain of the cheap crucifix grinding into his neck, and in his peril wondered how the sight of the object itself would affect the evil creature. Her strength was altogether superhuman, but as she continued her choking he reached feebly in his shirt and drew out

the metal symbol, snapping the chain and pulling it free.

At sight of the device the witch seemed struck with panic, and her grip relaxed long enough to give Gilman a chance to break it entirely. He pulled the steel-like claws from his neck, and would have dragged the beldame over the edge of the gulf had not the claws received a fresh access of strength and closed in again. This time he resolved to reply in kind, and his own hands reached out for the creature's throat. Before she saw what he was doing he had the chain of the crucifix twisted about her neck, and a moment later he had tightened it enough to cut off her breath. During her last struggle he felt something bite at his ankle, and saw that Brown Jenkin had come to her aid. With one savage kick he sent the morbidity over the edge of the gulf and heard it whimper on some level far below.

Whether he had killed the ancient crone he did not know, but he let her rest on the floor where she had fallen. Then, as he turned away, he saw on the table a sight which nearly snapped the last thread of his reason. Brown Jenkin, tough of sinew and with four tiny hands of daemoniac dexterity, had been busy while the witch was throttling him, and his efforts had been in vain. What he had prevented the knife from doing to the victim's chest, the yellow fangs of the furry blasphemy had done to a wrist—and the bowl so lately on the floor stood full beside the small lifeless body.

In his dream-delirium Gilman heard the hellish, alien-rhythmed chant of the Sabbat coming from an infinite distance, and knew the black man must be there. Confused memories mixed themselves with his mathematics, and he believed his subconscious mind held the angles which he needed to guide him back to the normal world—alone and unaided for the first time. He felt sure he was in the immemorially sealed loft above his own room, but whether he could ever escape through the slanting floor or the long-stopped egress he doubted greatly. Besides, would not an escape from a dream-loft bring him merely into a dream-house—an abnormal projection of the actual place he sought? He was wholly bewildered as to the relation betwixt dream and reality in all his experiences.

The passage through the vague abysses would be frightful, for the Walpurgis-rhythm would be vibrating, and at last he would have to hear that hitherto veiled cosmic pulsing which he so mortally dreaded. Even now he could detect a low, monstrous shaking whose tempo he suspected all too well. At Sabbat-time it always mounted and reached through to the worlds to summon the initiate to nameless rites. Half the chants of the Sabbat were patterned on this faintly overheard pulsing which no earthly ear could endure in its unveiled spatial fulness. Gilman wondered, too, whether he could trust his instinct to take him back to the right part of space. How could he be sure he would not land on that green-litten hillside of a far planet, on the tessellated terrace above the city of tentacled monsters somewhere beyond the galaxy, or in the spiral black vortices of that ultimate void of Chaos wherein reigns the mindless daemon-sultan Azathoth?

Just before he made the plunge the violet light went out and left him in utter blackness. The witch—old Keziah—Nahab—that must have meant her death. And mixed with the distant chant of the Sabbat and the whimpers of Brown Jenkin in the gulf below he thought he heard another and wilder whine from unknown depths. Joe Mazurewicz—the prayers against the Crawling Chaos now turning to an inexplicably triumphant shriek—worlds of sardonic actuality impinging on vortices of febrile dream—Iä! Shub-Niggurath! The Goat with a Thousand Young. . . .

They found Gilman on the floor of his queerly angled old garret room long before dawn, for the terrible cry had brought Desrochers and Choynski and Dombrowski and Mazurewicz at once, and had even wakened the soundly sleeping Elwood in his chair. He was alive, and with open, staring eyes, but seemed largely unconscious. On his throat were the marks of murderous hands, and on his left ankle was a distressing rat-bite. His clothing was badly rumpled, and Joe's crucifix was missing. Elwood trembled, afraid even to speculate on what new form his friend's sleep-walking had taken. Mazurewicz seemed half-dazed because of a "sign" he said he had had in response to his prayers, and he crossed himself frantically when the squealing and whimpering of a rat sounded from beyond the slanting partition.

When the dreamer was settled on his couch in Elwood's room they sent for Dr. Malkowski—a local practitioner who would repeat no tales where they might prove embarrassing—and he gave Gilman two hypodermic injections which caused him to relax in something like natural drowsiness. During the day the patient regained consciousness at times and whispered his newest dream disjointedly to Elwood. It was a painful process, and at its very start brought out a fresh and disconcerting fact.

Gilman—whose ears had so lately possessed an abnormal sensitiveness—was now stone deaf. Dr. Malkowski, summoned again in haste, told Elwood that both ear-drums were ruptured, as if by the impact of some stupendous sound intense beyond all human conception or endurance. How such a sound could have been heard in the last few hours without arousing all the Miskatonic Valley was more than the honest physician could say.

Elwood wrote his part of the colloquy on paper, so that a fairly easy communication was maintained. Neither knew what to make of the whole chaotic business, and decided it would be better if they thought as little as possible about it. Both, though, agreed that they must leave this ancient and accursed house as soon as it could be arranged. Evening papers spoke of a police raid on some curious revellers in a ravine beyond Meadow Hill just before dawn, and mentioned that the white stone there was an object of age-long superstitious regard. Nobody had been caught, but among the scattering fugitives had been glimpsed a huge negro. In another column it was stated that no trace of the missing child Ladislas Wolejko had been found.

The crowning horror came that very night. Elwood will never forget it, and was forced to stay out of college the rest of the term because of the resulting nervous breakdown. He had thought he heard rats in the partitions all the evening, but paid little attention to them. Then, long after both he and Gilman had retired, the atrocious shrieking began. Elwood jumped up, turned on the lights, and rushed over to his guest's couch. The occupant was emitting sounds of veritably inhuman nature, as if racked by some torment beyond description. He was writhing under the bedclothes, and a great red stain was beginning to appear on the blankets.

Elwood scarcely dared to touch him, but gradually the screaming and writhing subsided. By this time Dombrowski, Choynski, Desrochers, Mazurewicz, and the top-floor lodger were all crowding into the doorway, and the landlord had sent his wife back to telephone for Dr. Malkowski. Everybody shrieked when a large rat-like form suddenly jumped out from beneath the ensanguined bedclothes and scuttled across the floor to a fresh, open hole close by. When the doctor arrived and began to pull down those frightful covers Walter Gilman was dead.

It would be barbarous to do more than suggest what had killed Gilman. There had been virtually a tunnel through his body—something had eaten his heart out. Dombrowski, frantic at the failure of his constant rat-poisoning efforts, cast aside all thought of his lease and within a week had moved with all his older lodgers to a dingy but less ancient house in Walnut Street. The worst thing for a while was keeping Joe Mazurewicz quiet; for the brooding loomfixer would never stay sober, and was constantly whining and muttering about spectral and terrible things.

It seems that on that last hideous night Joe had stooped to look at the crimson rat-tracks which led from Gilman's couch to the nearby hole. On the carpet they were very indistinct, but a piece of open flooring intervened between the carpet's edge and the base-board. There Mazurewicz had found something monstrous—or thought he had, for no one else could quite agree with him despite the undeniable queerness of the prints. The tracks on the flooring were certainly vastly unlike the average prints of a rat, but even Choynski and Desrochers would not admit that they were like the prints of four tiny human hands.

The house was never rented again. As soon as Dombrowski left it the pall of its final desolation began to descend, for people shunned it both on account of its old reputation and because of the new foetid odour. Perhaps the ex-landlord's rat-poison had worked after all, for not long after his departure the place became a neighbourhood nuisance. Health officials traced the smell to the closed spaces above and beside the eastern garret room, and agreed that the number of dead rats must be enormous. They decided, however, that it was not worth their while to hew open and disinfect the long-sealed spaces; for the foetor would soon be over, and the locality was not one which encouraged fastidious standards. Indeed, there were always vague local tales of unexplained stenches upstairs in the Witch House just after May-Eve and Hallowmass. The neighbours grumblingly acquiesced in the inertia—but the foetor none the less formed an additional count against the place. Toward the last the house was condemned as an habitation by the building inspector.

Gilman's dreams and their attendant circumstances have never been explained. Elwood, whose thoughts on the entire episode are sometimes almost maddening, came back to college the next autumn and graduated in the following June. He found the spectral gossip of the town much diminished, and it is indeed a fact that—notwithstanding certain reports of a ghostly tittering in the deserted house which lasted almost as long as that edifice itself—no fresh appearances either of old Keziah or of Brown Jenkin have been muttered of since Gilman's death. It is rather fortunate that Elwood was not in Arkham in that later year when certain events abruptly renewed the local whispers about elder horrors. Of course he heard about the matter afterward and suffered untold torments of black and bewildered speculation; but even that was not as bad as actual nearness and several possible sights would have been.

In March, 1931, a gale wrecked the roof and great chimney of the vacant Witch House, so that a chaos of crumbling bricks, blackened, moss-grown shingles, and rotting planks and timbers crashed down into the loft and broke through the floor beneath. The whole attic story was choked with debris from above, but no one took the trouble to touch the mess before the inevitable razing of the decrepit structure. That ultimate step came in the following December, and it was when Gilman's old room was cleared out by reluctant, apprehensive workmen that the gossip began.

Among the rubbish which had crashed through the ancient slanting ceiling were several things which made the workmen pause and call in the police. Later the police in turn called in the coroner and several professors from the university. There were bones—badly crushed and splintered, but clearly recognisable as human—whose manifestly modern date conflicted puzzlingly with the remote period at which their only possible lurking-place, the low, slant-floored loft overhead, had supposedly been sealed from all human access. The coroner's physician decided that some belonged to a small child, while certain others—found mixed with shreds of rotten brownish cloth—belonged to a rather undersized, bent female of advanced years. Careful sifting of debris also disclosed many tiny bones of rats caught in the collapse, as well as older rat-bones gnawed by small fangs in a fashion now and then highly productive of controversy and reflection.

Other objects found included the mingled fragments of many books and papers, together with a yellowish dust left from the total disintegration of still older books and papers. All, without exception, appeared to deal with black magic in its most advanced and horrible forms; and the evidently recent date of certain items is still a mystery as unsolved as that of the modern human bones. An even greater mystery is the absolute homogeneity of the crabbed, archaic writing found on a wide range of papers whose conditions and watermarks suggest age differences of at least 150 to 200 years. To some, though, the greatest mystery of all is the variety of utterly inexplicable objects—objects whose shapes, materials, types of workmanship, and purposes baffle all conjecture—found scattered amidst the wreckage in evidently diverse states of injury. One of these things—which excited several Miskatonic professors profoundly—is a badly damaged monstrosity plainly resembling the strange image which Gilman gave to the college museum, save that it is larger, wrought of some peculiar bluish stone instead of metal, and possessed of a singularly angled pedestal with undecipherable hieroglyphics.

Archaeologists and anthropologists are still trying to explain the bizarre designs chased on a crushed bowl of light metal whose inner side bore ominous brownish stains when found. Foreigners and credulous grandmothers are equally garrulous about the modern nickel crucifix with broken chain mixed in the rubbish and shiveringly identified by Joe Mazurewicz as that which he had given poor Gilman many years before. Some believe this crucifix was dragged up to the sealed loft by rats, while others think it must have been on the floor in some corner of Gilman's old room all the time. Still others, including Joe himself, have theories too wild and fantastic for sober credence.

When the slanting wall of Gilman's room was torn out, the once sealed triangular space between that partition and the house's north wall was found to contain much less structural debris, even in proportion to its size, than the room itself; though it had a ghastly layer of older materials which paralysed the wreckers with horror. In brief, the floor was a veritable ossuary of the bones of small children—some fairly modern, but others extending back in infinite gradations to a period so remote that crumbling was almost complete. On this deep bony layer rested a knife of great size, obvious antiquity, and grotesque, ornate, and exotic design—above which the debris was piled.

In the midst of this debris, wedged between a fallen plank and a cluster of cemented bricks from the ruined chimney,

was an object destined to cause more bafflement, veiled fright, and openly superstitious talk in Arkham than anything else discovered in the haunted and accursed building. This object was the partly crushed skeleton of a huge, diseased rat, whose abnormalities of form are still a topic of debate and source of singular reticence among the members of Miskatonic's department of comparative anatomy. Very little concerning this skeleton has leaked out, but the workmen who found it whisper in shocked tones about the long, brownish hairs with which it was associated.

The bones of the tiny paws, it is rumoured, imply prehensile characteristics more typical of a diminutive monkey than of a rat; while the small skull with its savage yellow fangs is of the utmost anomalousness, appearing from certain angles like a miniature, monstrously degraded parody of a human skull. The workmen crossed themselves in fright when they came upon this blasphemy, but later burned candles of gratitude in St. Stanislaus' Church because of the shrill, ghostly tittering they felt they would never hear again.

THE END

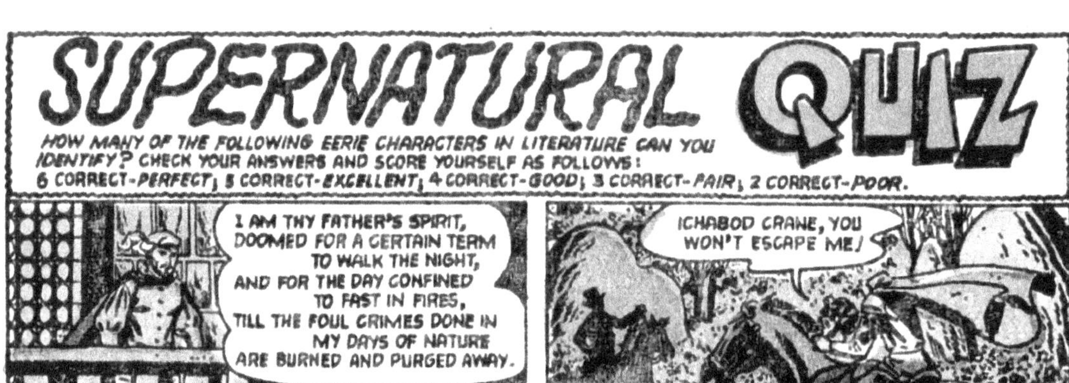
SUPERNATURAL QUIZ
HOW MANY OF THE FOLLOWING EERIE CHARACTERS IN LITERATURE CAN YOU IDENTIFY? CHECK YOUR ANSWERS AND SCORE YOURSELF AS FOLLOWS:
6 CORRECT-PERFECT; 5 CORRECT-EXCELLENT; 4 CORRECT-GOOD; 3 CORRECT-FAIR; 2 CORRECT-POOR.
I AM THY FATHER'S SPIRIT, DOOMED FOR A CERTAIN TERM TO WALK THE NIGHT, AND FOR THE DAY CONFINED TO FAST IN FIRES, TILL THE FOUL CRIMES DONE IN MY DAYS OF NATURE ARE BURNED AND PURGED AWAY.
ANSWER- THE GHOST OF HAMLET -- HAMLET BY WILLIAM SHAKESPEARE.

ICHABOD CRANE, YOU WON'T ESCAPE ME!
ANSWER- THE HEADLESS HORSEMAN -- THE LEGEND OF SLEEPY HOLLOW BY WASHINGTON IRVING.

EEEEYAAH!

ANSWER- THE GHOST SHIP THE FLYING DUTCHMAN -- THE FLYING DUTCHMAN, OPERA BY RICHARD WAGNER.

DOUBLE, DOUBLE, TOIL AND TROUBLE, FIRE BURN AND CAULDRON BUBBLE.
ANSWER- THE THREE WITCHES -- MACBETH BY WILLIAM SHAKESPEARE.

HERE ON EARTH I WILL DO YOUR BIDDING! LATER IN THE UNDERWORLD YOU WILL WAIT ON ME!
ANSWER- MEPHISTOPHELES -- FAUST BY JOHANN WOLFGANG VON GOETHE.

MY LAND IS THREATENED! MY PEOPLE ARE ABOUT TO BE ATTACKED BY THE PHILISTINES! IF YOU COULD BRING THE DEAD KING SAMUEL BACK HE COULD ADVISE ME!
SO, PROUD KING, FIRST YOU BANISH ALL NECROMANCERS AND NOW YOU COME CRAWLING FOR HELP!
ANSWER- THE WITCH OF ENDOR -- THE BIBLE.

DIG ME NO GRAVE
BY ROBERT E. HOWARD

THE THUNDER OF MY OLD-FASHIONED door-knocker, reverberating eerily through the house, roused me from a restless and nightmare-haunted sleep. I looked out the window. In the last light of the sinking moon, the white face of my friend John Conrad looked up at me.

"May I come up, Kirowan?" His voice was shaky and strained.

"Certainly!" I sprang out of bed and pulled on a bath-robe as I heard him enter the front door and ascend the stairs.

A moment later he stood before me, and in the light which I had turned on I saw his hands tremble and noticed the unnatural pallor of his face.

"Old John Grimlan died an hour ago," he said abruptly.

"Indeed? I had not known that he was ill."

"It was a sudden, virulent attack of peculiar nature, a sort of seizure somewhat akin to epilepsy. He has been subject to such spells of late years, you know."

I nodded. I knew something of the old hermit-like man who had lived in his great dark house on the hill; indeed, I had once witnessed one of his strange seizures, and I had been appalled at the writhings, howlings and yammerings of the wretch, who had groveled on the earth like a wounded snake, gibbering terrible curses and black blasphemies until his voice broke in a wordless screaming which spattered his lips with foam. Seeing this, I understood why people in old times looked on such victims as men possessed by demons.

"——some hereditary taint," Conrad was saying. "Old John doubtless fell heir to some ingrown weakness brought on by some loathsome disease, which was his heritage from perhaps a remote ancestor—such things occasionally happen. Or else—well, you know old John himself pried about in the mysterious parts of the earth, and wandered all over the East in his younger days. It is quite possible that he was infected with some obscure malady in his wanderings. There are still many unclassified diseases in Africa and the Orient."

"But," said I, "you have not told me the reason for this sudden visit at this unearthly hour—for I notice that it is past midnight."

My friend seemed rather confused.

"Well, the fact is that John Grimlan died alone, except for myself. He refused to receive any medical aid of any sort, and in the last few moments when it was evident that he was dying, and I was prepared to go for some sort of help in spite of him, he set up such a howling and screaming that I could not refuse his passionate pleas—which were that he should not be left to die alone.

"I have seen men die," added Conrad, wiping the perspiration from his pale brow, "but the death of John Grimlan was the most fearful I have ever seen."

"He suffered a great deal?"

"He appeared to be in much physical agony, but this was mostly submerged by some monstrous mental or psychic suffering. The fear in his distended eyes and his screams transcended any conceivable earthly terror. I tell you, Kirowan, Grimlan's fright was greater and deeper than the ordinary fear of the Beyond shown by a man of ordinarily evil life."

I shifted restlessly. The dark implications of this statement sent a chill of nameless apprehension trickling down my spine.

"I know the country people always claimed that in his youth he sold his soul to the Devil, and that his sudden epileptic attacks were merely a visible sign of the Fiend's power over him; but such talk is foolish, of course, and belongs in the Dark Ages. We all know that John Grimlan's life was a peculiarly evil and vicious one, even toward his last days. With good reason he was universally detested and feared, for I never heard of his doing a single good act. You were his only friend."

"And that was a strange friendship," said Conrad. "I was attracted to him by his unusual powers, for despite his bestial nature, John Grimlan was a highly educated man, a deeply cultured man. He had dipped deep into occult studies, and I first met him in this manner; for as you know, I have always been strongly interested in these lines of research myself.

"But, in this as in all other things, Grimlan was evil and perverse. He had ignored the white side of the occult and delved into the darker, grimmer phases of it—into devil-worship, and voodoo and Shintoism. His knowledge of these foul arts and sciences was immense and unholy. And to hear him tell of his researches and experiments was to know such horror and repulsion as a venomous reptile might inspire. For there had been no depths to which he had not sunk, and some things he only hinted at, even to me. I tell you, Kirowan, it is easy to laugh at tales of the black world of the unknown, when one is in pleasant company under the bright sunlight, but had you sat at ungodly hours in the silent bizarre library of John Grimlan and looked on the ancient musty volumes and listened to his grisly talk as I did, your

tongue would have cloven to your palate with sheer horror as mine did, and the supernatural would have seemed very real and near to you—as it seemed to me!"

"But in God's name, man!" I cried, for the tension was growing unbearable; "come to the point and tell me what you want of me."

"I want you to come with me to John Grimlan's house and help carry out his outlandish instructions in regard to his body."

I HAD NO LIKING FOR THE ADVENTURE, but I dressed hurriedly, an occasional shudder of premonition shaking me. Once fully clad, I followed Conrad out of the house and up the silent road which led to the house of John Grimlan. The road wound uphill, and all the way, looking upward and forward, I could see that great grim house perched like a bird of evil on the crest of the hill, bulking black and stark against the stars. In the west pulsed a single dull red smear where the young moon had just sunk from view behind the low black hills. The whole night seemed full of brooding evil, and the persistent swishing of a bat's wings somewhere overhead caused my taut nerves to jerk and thrum. To drown the quick pounding of my own heart, I said:

"Do you share the belief so many hold, that John Grimlan was mad?"

We strode on several paces before Conrad answered, seemingly with a strange reluctance, "But for one incident, I would say no man was ever saner. But one night in his study, he seemed suddenly to break all bonds of reason.

"He had discoursed for hours on his favorite subject—black magic—when suddenly he cried, as his face lit with a weird unholy glow: 'Why should I sit here babbling such child's prattle to you? These voodoo rituals—these Shinto sacrifices—feathered snakes—goats without horns—black leopard cults—bah! Filth and dust that the wind blows away! Dregs of the real Unknown—the deep mysteries! Mere echoes from the Abyss!

"'I could tell you things that would shatter your paltry brain! I could breathe into your ear names that would wither you like a burnt weed! What do you know of Yog-Sothoth, of Kathulos and the sunken cities? None of these names is even included in your mythologies. Not even in your dreams have you glimpsed the black cyclopean walls of Koth, or shriveled before the noxious winds that blow from Yuggoth!

"'But I will not blast you lifeless with my black wisdom! I cannot expect your infantile brain to bear what mine holds. Were you as old as I—had you seen, as I have seen, kingdoms crumble and generations pass away—had you gathered as ripe grain the dark secrets of the centuries——'

"He was raving away, his wildly lit face scarcely human in appearance, and suddenly, noting my evident bewilderment, he burst into a horrible cackling laugh.

"'Gad!' he cried in a voice and accent strange to me, 'methinks I've frighted ye, and certes, it is not to be marveled at, sith ye be but a naked savage in the arts of life, after all. Ye think I be old, eh? Why, ye gaping lout, ye'd drop dead were I to divulge the generations of men I've known——'

"But at this point such horror overcame me that I fled from him as from an adder, and his high-pitched, diabolical laughter followed me out of the shadowy house. Some days later I received a letter apologizing for his manner and ascribing it candidly—too candidly—to drugs. I did not believe it, but I renewed our relations, after some hesitation."

"It sounds like utter madness," I muttered.

"Yes," admitted Conrad, hesitantly. "But—Kirowan, have you ever seen anyone who knew John Grimlan in his youth?"

I shook my head.

"I have been at pains to inquire about him discreetly," said Conrad. "He has lived here—with the exception of mysterious absences often for months at a time—for twenty years. The older villagers remember distinctly when he first came and took over that old house on the hill, and they all say that in the intervening years he seems not to have aged perceptibly. When he came here he looked just as he does now—or did, up to the moment of his death—of the appearance of a man about fifty.

"I met old Von Boehnk in Vienna, who said he knew Grimlan when a very young man studying in Berlin, fifty years ago, and he expressed astonishment that the old man was still living; for he said at that time Grimlan seemed to be about fifty years of age."

I gave an incredulous exclamation, seeing the implication toward which the conversation was trending.

"Nonsense! Professor Von Boehnk is past eighty himself, and liable to the errors of extreme age. He confused this man with another." Yet as I spoke, my flesh crawled unpleasantly and the hairs on my neck prickled.

"Well," shrugged Conrad, "here we are at the house."

THE HUGE PILE REARED UP MENACINGLY before us, and as we reached the front door a vagrant wind moaned through the near-by trees and I started foolishly as I again heard the ghostly beat of the bat's wings. Conrad turned a large key in the antique lock, and as we entered, a cold draft swept across us like a breath from the grave—moldy and cold. I shuddered.

We groped our way through a black hallway and into a study, and here Conrad lighted a candle, for no gas lights or electric lights were to be found in the house. I looked about me, dreading what the light might disclose, but the room, heavily tapestried and bizarrely furnished, was empty save for us two.

"Where—where is—*It?*" I asked in a husky whisper, from a throat gone dry.

"Upstairs," answered Conrad in a low voice, showing that the silence and mystery of the house had laid a spell on him also. "Upstairs, in the library where he died."

I glanced up involuntarily. Somewhere above our head, the lone master of this grim house was stretched out in his last sleep—silent, his white face set in a grinning mask of death. Panic swept over me and I fought for control. After all, it was merely the corpse of a wicked old man, who was past harming anyone—this argument rang hollowly in my brain like the words of a frightened child who is trying to reassure himself.

I turned to Conrad. He had taken a time-yellowed envelope from an inside pocket.

"This," he said, removing from the envelope several pages of closely written, time-yellowed parchment, "is, in effect, the last word of John Grimlan, though God alone knows how many years ago it was written. He gave it to me ten years ago, immediately after his return from Mongolia. It was shortly after this that he had his first seizure.

"This envelope he gave me, sealed, and he made me swear that I would hide it carefully, and that I would not open it until he was dead, when I was to read the contents and follow their directions exactly. More, he made me swear that no matter what he said or did after giving me the envelope, I would go ahead as first directed. 'For,' he said with a fearful smile, 'the flesh is weak but I am a man of my word, and though I might, in a moment of weakness, wish to retract, it is far, far too late now. You may never understand the matter, but you are to do as I have said.'"

"Well?"

"Well," again Conrad wiped his brow, "tonight as he lay writhing in his death-agonies, his wordless howls were mingled with frantic admonitions to me to bring him the envelope and destroy it before his eyes! As he yammered this, he forced himself up on his elbows and with eyes starting and hair standing straight up on his head, he screamed at me in a manner to chill the blood. And he was shrieking for me to destroy the envelope, not to open it; and once he howled in his delirium for me to hew his body into pieces and scatter the bits to the four winds of heaven!"

An uncontrollable exclamation of horror escaped my dry lips.

"At last," went on Conrad, "I gave in. Remembering his commands ten years ago, I at first stood firm, but at last, as his screeches grew unbearably desperate, I turned to go for the envelope, even though that meant leaving him alone. But as I turned, with one last fearful convulsion in which blood-flecked foam flew from his writhing lips, the life went from his twisted body in a single great wrench."

He fumbled at the parchment.

"I am going to carry out my promise. The directions herein seem fantastic and may be the whims of a disordered mind, but I gave my word. They are, briefly, that I place his corpse on the great black ebony table in his library, with seven black candles burning about him. The doors and windows are to be firmly closed and fastened. Then, in the darkness which precedes dawn, I am to read the formula, charm or spell which is contained in a smaller, sealed envelope inside the first, and which I have not yet opened."

"But is that all?" I cried. "No provisions as to the disposition of his fortune his estate—or his corpse?"

"Nothing. In his will, which I have seen elsewhere, he leaves estate and fortune to a certain oriental gentleman named in the document as—Malik Tous!»

"What!" I cried, shaken to my soul. "Conrad, this is madness heaped on madness! Malik Tous—good God! No mortal man was ever so named! That is the title of the foul god worshipped by the mysterious Yezidees—they of Mount Alamout the Accursed—whose Eight Brazen Towers rise in the mysterious wastes of deep Asia. His idolatrous symbol is the brazen peacock. And the Muhammadans, who hate his demon-worshipping devotees, say he is the essence of the evil of all the universes—the Prince of Darkness—Ahriman—the old Serpent—the veritable Satan! And you say Grimlan names this mythical demon in his will?"

"It is the truth," Conrad's throat was dry. "And look—he has scribbled a strange line at the corner of this parchment: 'Dig me no grave; I shall not need one.'"

Again a chill wandered down my spine.

"In God's name," I cried in a kind of frenzy, "let us get this incredible business over with!"

"I think a drink might help," answered Conrad, moistening his lips. "It seems to me I've seen Grimlan go into this cabinet for wine——" He bent to the door of an ornately carved mahogany cabinet, and after some difficulty opened it.

"No wine here," he said disappointedly, "and if ever I felt the need of stimulants—what's this?"

He drew out a roll of parchment, dusty, yellowed and half covered with spiderwebs. Everything in that grim house seemed, to my nervously excited senses, fraught with mysterious meaning and import, and I leaned over his shoulder as he unrolled it.

"It's a record of peerage," he said, "such a chronicle of births, deaths and so forth, as the old families used to keep, in the Sixteenth Century and earlier."

"What's the name?" I asked.

He scowled over the dim scrawls, striving to master the faded, archaic script.

"G-r-y-m—I've got it—Grymlann, of course. It's the records of old John's family—the Grymlanns of Toad's-heath Manor, Suffolk—what an outlandish name for an estate! Look at the last entry."

Together we read, "John Grymlann, borne, March 10, 1630." And then we both cried out. Under this entry was freshly written, in a strange scrawling hand, "Died, March 10, 1930." Below this there was a seal of black wax, stamped with a strange design, something like a peacock with a spreading tail.

Conrad stared at me speechless, all the color ebbed from his face. I shook myself with the rage engendered by fear.

"It's the hoax of a madman!" I shouted. "The stage has been set with such great care that the actors have overstepped themselves. Whoever they are, they have heaped up so many incredible effects as to nullify them. It's all a very stupid, very dull drama of illusion."

And even as I spoke, icy sweat stood out on my body and I shook as with an ague. With a wordless motion Conrad turned toward the stairs, taking up a large candle from a mahogany table.

"It was understood, I suppose," he whispered, "that I should go through with this ghastly matter alone; but I had not the moral courage, and now I'm glad I had not."

★ ★ ★

A STILL HORROR BROODED OVER THE silent house as we went up the stairs. A faint breeze stole in from somewhere and set the heavy velvet hangings rustling, and I visualized stealthy taloned fingers drawing aside the tapestries, to fix red gloating eyes upon us. Once I thought I heard the indistinct clumping of monstrous feet somewhere above us, but it must have been the heavy pounding of my own heart.

The stairs debouched into a wide dark corridor, in which our feeble candle cast a faint gleam which but illuminated our pale faces and made the shadows seem darker by comparison. We stopped at a heavy door, and I heard Conrad's breath draw in sharply as a man's will when he braces himself physically or mentally. I involuntarily clenched my fists until the nails bit into the palms; then Conrad thrust the door open.

A sharp cry escaped his lips. The candle dropped from his nerveless fingers and went out. The library of John Grimlan was ablaze with light, though the whole house had been in darkness when we entered it.

This light came from seven black candles placed at regular intervals about the great ebony table. On this table, between the candles—I had braced myself against the sight. Now in the face of the mysterious illumination and the sight of the thing on the table, my resolution nearly gave way. John Grimlan had been unlovely in life; in death he was hideous. Yes, he was hideous even though his face was mercifully covered with the same curious silken robe, which, worked in fantastic bird-like designs, covered his whole body except the crooked claw-like hands and the bare withered feet.

A strangling sound came from Conrad. "My God!" he whispered; "what is this? I laid his body out on the table and placed the candles about it, but I did not light them, nor did I place that robe over the body! And there were bedroom slippers on his feet when I left——»

He halted suddenly. We were not alone in the deathroom.

At first we had not seen him, as he sat in the great armchair in a farther nook of a corner, so still that he seemed a part of the shadows cast by the heavy tapestries. As my eyes fell upon him, a violent shuddering shook me and a feeling akin to nausea racked the pit of my stomach. My first impression was of vivid, oblique yellow eyes which gazed unwinkingly at us. Then the man rose and made a deep salaam, and we saw that he was an oriental. Now when I strive to etch him clearly in my mind, I can resurrect no plain image of him. I only remember those piercing eyes and the yellow, fantastic robe he wore.

We returned his salute mechanically and he spoke in a low, refined voice, "Gentlemen, I crave your pardon! I have made so free as to light the candles—shall we not proceed with the business pertaining to our mutual friend?"

He made a slight gesture toward the silent bulk on the table. Conrad nodded, evidently unable to speak. The thought flashed through our minds at the same time, that this man had also been given a sealed envelope—but how had he come to the Grimlan house so quickly? John Grimlan had been dead scarcely two hours and to the best of our knowledge no one knew of his demise but ourselves. And how had he got into the locked and bolted house?

The whole affair was grotesque and unreal in the extreme. We did not even introduce ourselves or ask the stranger his name. He took charge in a matter-of-fact way, and so under the spell of horror and illusion were we that we moved dazedly, involuntarily obeying his suggestions, given us in a low, respectful tone.

I found myself standing on the left side of the table, looking across its grisly burden at Conrad. The oriental stood with arms folded and head bowed at the head of the table, nor did it then strike me as being strange that he should stand there, instead of Conrad who was to read what Grimlan had written. I found my gaze drawn to the figure worked on the breast of the stranger's robe, in black silk—a curious figure, somewhat resembling a peacock and somewhat resembling a bat, or a flying dragon. I noted with a start that the same design was worked on the robe covering the corpse.

The doors had been locked, the windows fastened down. Conrad, with a shaky hand, opened the inner envelope and fluttered open the parchment sheets contained therein. These sheets seemed much older than those containing the instructions to Conrad, in the larger envelope. Conrad began to read in a monotonous drone which had the effect of hypnosis on the hearer; so at times the candles grew dim in my gaze and the room and its occupants swam strange and monstrous, veiled and distorted like an hallucination. Most of what he read was gibberish; it meant nothing; yet the sound of it and the archaic style of it filled me with an intolerable horror.

"To ye contract elsewhere recorded, I, John Grymlann, herebye sweare by ye Name of ye Nameless One to keep goode faithe. Wherefore do I now write in blood these wordes spoken to me in thys grim & silent chamber in ye dedde citie of Koth, whereto no mortal manne hath attained but mee. These same wordes now writ down by mee to be rede over my bodie at ye appointed tyme to fulfill my parte of ye bargain which I entered intoe of mine own free will & knowledge beinge of rite mynd & fiftie years of age this yeare of 1680, A.D. Here begynneth ye incantation:

"Before manne was, ye Elder ones were, & even yet their lord dwelleth amonge ye shadows to which if a manne sette his foote he maye not turn vpon his track."

The words merged into a barbaric gibberish as Conrad stumbled through an unfamiliar language—a language faintly suggesting the Phenician, but shuddery with the touch of a hideous antiquity beyond any remembered earthly tongue. One of the candles flickered and went out. I made a move to relight it, but a motion from the silent oriental stayed me. His eyes burned into mine, then shifted back to the still form on the table.

The manuscript had shifted back into its archaic English.

«——And ye mortal which gaineth to ye black citadels of Koth & speaks with ye Darke Lord whose face is hidden, for a price maye he gain hys heartes desire, ryches & knowledge beyond countinge & lyffe beyond mortal span even two hundred & fiftie yeares."

Again Conrad's voice trailed off into unfamiliar gutturals. Another candle went out.

«——Let not ye mortal flynche as ye tyme draweth nigh for payement & ye fires of Hell laye hold vpon ye vytals as the sign of reckoninge. For ye Prince of Darkness taketh hys due in ye endde & he is not to bee cozened. What ye have promised, that shall ye deliver. *Augantha na shuba*——»

At the first sound of those barbaric accents, a cold hand of terror locked about my throat. My frantic eyes shot to the candles and I was not surprized to see another flicker out. Yet there was no hint of any draft to stir the heavy black hangings. Conrad's voice wavered; he drew his hand across his throat, gagging momentarily. The eyes of the oriental never altered.

«——Amonge ye sonnes of men glide strange shadows for ever. Men see ye tracks of ye talones but not ye feete that make them. Over ye souls of men spread great black wingges. There is but one Black Master though men calle hym Sathanas & Beelzebub & Apolleon & Ahriman & Malik Tous——»

Mists of horror engulfed me. I was dimly aware of Conrad's voice droning on and on, both in English and in that other fearsome tongue whose horrific import I scarcely dared try to guess. And with stark fear clutching at my heart, I saw the candles go out, one by one. And with each flicker, as the gathering gloom darkened about us, my horror mounted. I could not speak, I could not move; my distended eyes were fixed with agonized intensity on the remaining candle. The silent oriental at the head of that ghastly table was included in my fear. He had not moved nor spoken, but under his drooping lids, his eyes burned with devilish triumph; I knew that beneath his inscrutable exterior he was gloating fiendishly—but why—*why?*

"With stark fear clutching at his heart he saw the candles go out, one by one."

But I *knew* that the moment the extinguishing of the last candle plunged the room into utter darkness, some nameless, abominable thing would take place. Conrad

was approaching the end. His voice rose to the climax in gathering crescendo.

"Approacheth now ye moment of payement. Ye ravens are flying. Ye bats winge against ye skye. There are skulls in ye starres. Ye soul & ye bodie are promised and shall bee delivered uppe. Not to ye dust agayne nor ye elements from which springe lyfe———»

The candle flickered slightly. I tried to scream, but my mouth gaped to a soundless yammering. I tried to flee, but I stood frozen, unable even to close my eyes.

«———Ye abysse yawns & ye debt is to paye. Ye light fayles, ye shadows gather. There is no god but evil; no lite but darkness; no hope but doom———»

A hollow groan resounded through the room. *It seemed to come from the robe-covered thing on the table!* That robe twitched fitfully.

"Oh winges in ye black darke!"

I started violently; a faint swish sounded in the gathering shadows. The stir of the dark hangings? It sounded like the rustle of gigantic wings.

"Oh redde eyes in ye shadows! What is promised, what is writ in bloode is fulfilled! Ye lite is gulfed in blackness! Ya—Koth!"

The last candle went out suddenly and a ghastly unhuman cry that came not from my lips or from Conrad's burst unbearably forth. Horror swept over me like a black icy wave; in the blind dark I heard myself screaming terribly. Then with a swirl and a great rush of wind something swept the room, flinging the hangings aloft and dashing chairs and tables crashing to the floor. For an instant an intolerable odor burned our nostrils, a low hideous tittering mocked us in the blackness; then silence fell like a shroud.

Somehow, Conrad found a candle and lighted it. The faint glow showed us the room in fearful disarray—showed us each other's ghastly faces—and showed us the black ebony table—empty! The doors and windows were locked as they had been, but the oriental was gone—and so was the corpse of John Grimlan.

Shrieking like damned men we broke down the door and fled frenziedly down the well-like staircase where the darkness seemed to clutch at us with clammy black fingers. As we tumbled down into the lower hallway, a lurid glow cut the darkness and the scent of burning wood filled our nostrils.

The outer doorway held momentarily against our frantic assault, then gave way and we hurtled into the outer starlight. Behind us the flames leaped up with a crackling roar as we fled down the hill. Conrad, glancing over his shoulder, halted suddenly, wheeled and flung up his arms like a madman, and screamed, "Soul and body he sold to Malik Tous, who is Satan, two hundred and fifty years ago! This was the night of payment—and my God—look! *Look!* The Fiend has claimed his own!"

I looked, frozen with horror. Flames had enveloped the whole house with appalling swiftness, and now the great mass was etched against the shadowed sky, a crimson inferno. And above the holocaust hovered a gigantic black shadow like a monstrous bat, and from its dark clutch dangled a small white thing, like the body of a man, dangling limply. Then, even as we cried out in horror, it was gone and our dazed gaze met only the shuddering walls and blazing roof which crumpled into the flames with an earth-shaking roar.

THE END

CONTRIBUTORS

MICHAEL BUNKER is a *USA Today* Bestselling author, off-gridder, husband, and father of four children. He lives with his family in Central Texas where he reads and writes books…and occasionally tilts at windmills. In November of 2015, Variety Magazine announced that Michael had sold a film/tv option for his bestselling novel *Pennsylvania* to Jorgensen Pictures.

K. VICTORIA CHASE is a graduate of Drexel University's MFA in Creative Writing program. In her day job, she edits products and papers for the US military. At night, Tori writes and independently publishes stories across the romance genre and freelances as a developmental editor. She loves HGTV shows, true crime podcasts, and traveling.

EDMUND VANCE COOKE (1866 – 1932) was a 19th- and 20th-century poet best remembered for his inspirational verse "How Did You Die?"

GARDNER FOX (1911 – 1986) was an American writer known best for creating numerous comic book characters for DC Comics. He is estimated to have written more than 4,000 comics stories,[4] including 1,500 for DC Comics. Fox was also a science fiction author and wrote many novels and short stories.

ROBERT E. HOWARD (1906 – 1936) was an American writer who wrote pulp fiction in a diverse range of genres. He created the character Conan the Barbarian and is regarded as the father of the sword and sorcery subgenre.

H. P. LOVECRAFT (1890 – 1937) was an American writer of weird, science, fantasy, and horror fiction. He is best known for his creation of the Cthulhu Mythos.

HERMAN MELVILLE (1819 – 1891) was an American novelist, short story writer, and poet of the American Renaissance period. Among his best-known works are *Moby-Dick, Typee,* and *Billy Budd, Sailor.* At the time of his death, Melville was no longer well known to the public, but the 1919 centennial of his birth was the starting point of a Melville revival. *Moby-Dick* eventually would be considered one of the great American novels.

KEVIN G. SUMMERS is the author of *Legendarium, The Man Who Shot John Wilkes Booth,* and *The Bleak December.*

BOOTH TARKINGTON (1869 – 1946) was an American novelist and dramatist best known for his novels The Magnificent Ambersons (1918) and Alice Adams (1921). He is one of only four novelists to win the Pulitzer Prize for Fiction more than once.